"I can't imagine how this happened, Saxon."

"Can't you, Gale?" Sax said quietly.

With unsteady fingers, she pushed back her hair. Sliding carefully off his lap, she began straightening her clothes while he looked on, the sardonic gleam in his eyes doing nothing at all to help the situation.

"No, I can't," she snapped. "I came downstairs because I thought someone was trying to burgle the place, and that's the only reason!"

"If you say so." He shrugged. "Can't blame me for getting the wrong idea, though, Gale. When a man and a woman living together alone share a candlelit dinner, and then meet again at midnight—when she's all soft and flushed, and her lips have that certain look about them, then a man would have to be a fool not to pick up his cue."

"I was *not* soft and flushed!" she argued, clutching her robe tightly around her. "And what's more, my lips didn't have any look at all about them."

"And I'm no fool, Gale."

Dear Reader,

Spellbinders! That's what we're striving for. The editors at Silhouette are determined to capture your imagination and win your heart with every single book we publish. Each month, six Special Editions are chosen with *you* in mind.

Our authors are our inspiration. Writers such as Nora Roberts, Tracy Sinclair, Kathleen Eagle, Carole Halston and Linda Howard—to name but a few—are masters at creating endearing characters and heartrending love stories. Their characters are everyday people—just like you and me—whose lives have been touched by love, whose dreams and desires suddenly come true!

So find a cozy, quiet place to read, and create your own special moment with a Silhouette Special Edition.

Sincerely,

The Editors
SILHOUETTE BOOKS

DIXIE
BROWNING
Belonging

Silhouette Special Edition

Published by Silhouette Books New York

America's Publisher of Contemporary Romance

To Mary Williams and Elizabeth Fox—
Three heads are better than one.

SILHOUETTE BOOKS
300 East 42nd St., New York, N.Y. 10017

Copyright © 1987 by Dixie Browning

ISBN: 0-373-09414-0

First Silhouette Books printing October 1987

America's Publisher of Contemporary Romance

Printed in the U.S.A.

DIXIE BROWNING

has written close to forty books for Silhouette since 1980. She is a charter member of the Romance Writers of America, and *Renegade Player* won a Golden Medallion in 1983. A charismatic lecturer, Dixie has toured extensively for Silhouette Books, participating in "How To Write A Romance" workshops all over the country.

Along with her writing, Dixie has been acclaimed as a watercolor painter, and was the first president of the Watercolor Society of North Carolina. She is currently president of Browning Artworks, Ltd., a gallery featuring fine crafts on Hatteras Island.

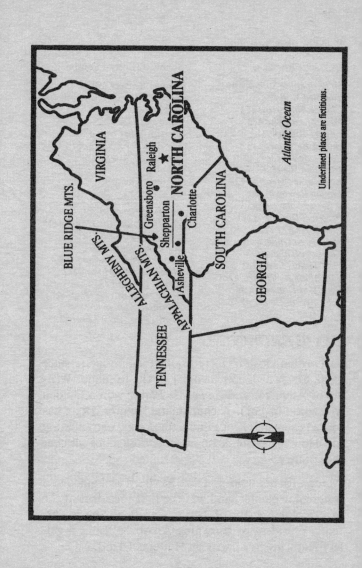

VIRGINIA

BLUE RIDGE MTS.

Greensboro Raleigh
★
NORTH CAROLINA

Shepparton

Asheville
Charlotte

ALLEGHENY MTS.

APPALACHIAN MTS.

TENNESSEE

SOUTH CAROLINA

GEORGIA

Atlantic Ocean

Underlined places are fictitious.

N

Chapter One

Saxon Evanshaw woke just before daybreak. He struggled from the bonds of a highly erotic dream and sat up, conscious of having reached two decisions during the night.

The first was that he wouldn't be asking Enid to marry him. There'd been times during the past few winters when he'd seriously considered settling down. At thirty-seven, he was getting too old to chase women, though he was a damned sight too young to do without them. Enid was a generous woman; he had a lot of respect for her. She'd hinted more than once that she wouldn't mind stepping up their relationship, but somehow he just couldn't see the two of them together for the long haul.

The second decision was that he was going back home.

Over breakfast, he broke the news to his partner, Jackson "Jay" Mathis, co-owner of Steppin' Creek Ranch.

"Figgered you'd be headed east any day now. You got that restless look to you, Dude."

"Quit trying to sound like Slim Pickens, Jay. Can you manage for a couple of weeks without me?"

"I managed to manage for forty-three years without you. Is it your dad? Any more news?"

Sax shook his head. Two days ago he'd had a note from an old friend from home, apologizing for not having written sooner. *I sort of thought you might be coming back home after your dad's stroke, but I guess you've been keeping tabs through the hospital and the nursing home. Damned shame, Sax. Your old man bailed us both out of many a patch of trouble back at St. Andrew's.*

The news had shaken Sax badly. He'd put through a call to the family physician and been conditionally reassured, but it hadn't been enough.

Damn Olivia! He could strangle the woman for not letting him know immediately. The post office had his forwarding address. He'd kept it up to date for the past eleven years.

There was no love lost between Sax and his father's second wife, Olivia Donner Evanshaw. She had been the reason he'd left home eleven years before and never gone back, but dammit, this was different.

"Dude?" Jay's gravelly drawl roused him from his deeply troubled thoughts.

"No, nothing more. I called the hospital and found out he's been transferred to a nursing home. That's a good sign, isn't it?" Sax looked at the lean, weathered man across the table from him. He'd won a half interest in Jay's run-down cattle ranch in a poker game the day they'd both gotten out of the coast guard. They'd tackled it together, working eighteen-hour days and seven-day weeks for the past five years. It was finally paying off.

"Sounds favorable to me, but then I don't know much about nursing homes and hospitals. I ain't ever had nothing a good dose o' salts or a rag dipped in turpentine wouldn't cure. O' course, with you Easterners, it's different. You'd throw your pinky outta joint crookin' it over a teacup."

Jay enjoyed playing the role of a redneck cowpoke when it suited him, but for once Sax failed to rise to the bait. Instead, he crossed to the electric coffee maker that sat so incongruously on top of the unused cast iron range and topped off his mug. "I booked a flight out of Amarillo. I can take the pickup, but then you'll be without it until I get back."

"I'll haul you in the chopper if'n I can find my red socks." Jay, who'd been flying search and rescue for the coast guard when Sax had first met him, was convinced he owed his life several times over to a pair of scarlet wool hunting socks. Saxon happened to know that Jay Mathis was a first-rate pilot with a sharp eye, a cool head and an unfortunate weakness for the cards.

After the older man had left, Sax took a look around the drafty kitchen. Tully, the cook, was out feeding the hens. He'd be back in a few minutes, and Sax didn't feel up to answering any questions about where he was going or why. The crew at Steppin' Creek had accepted the fact that he was a transplanted Easterner who, for reasons of his own, was willing to work hard for small returns.

Not even Jay knew all the details of Sax Evanshaw's background, although he'd come pretty close to guessing most of them. As for Sax's reasons for turning his back on his heritage, no one knew that. No one except himself and his father, and he doubted seriously that Richard Evanshaw had ever confided in anyone that he'd once called his own son a bastard.

Sax had been twenty-four when his mother had been killed in a fox-hunting accident. Richard's secretary, Olivia Donner, had continued to work quietly behind the scenes, and had slowly eased into the breach. Five months later, Richard had announced his plans to marry Olivia and adopt her fifteen-year-old son, Jeffry. Sax had been stunned.

Still mourning his mother's death, he'd struck out wildly. Richard had struck back. The pride and temper so typical of both men had carried them swiftly to the point of no return.

"For God's sake, Dad, you can't marry Olivia—she's your secretary! You're not thinking straight!"

"And as usual, you're not thinking at all. How many times do I have to tell you never to discuss a matter until you're in full possession of all the facts? Let it drop, Saxon."

"The hell I'll let it drop! I know all the facts I need to know. My mother's been dead just a few months and you're acting like a damned fool over another woman. Just because Olivia's been around so long, you seem to think—"

"That's enough!" The stocky, white-haired man had turned brick red. "You want facts? I'll give you facts! Olivia Donner has been more than a secretary to me since the first week she came to work here."

Sax could still remember the sick feeling of disbelief that had swept over him. "But that's been..."

"Sixteen years. I think it's past time I made it official."

"But she was still married then. She had a son."

"I have every reason to believe Jeff is mine. Olivia was in the process of getting a divorce sixteen years ago."

Shaken, Sax had rejected the idea at first. "I don't believe you. That—that baby-faced brat of hers is *my half brother*? There's no way I'll believe that. I just hope Mother died without ever learning what a real bastard you are."

"Your mother lived her life and I lived mine, and it's none of your damned business. But before you throw around any more ugly words, maybe you'd better get a few more facts straight. Your mother was having her own fun long before Olivia and I ever met. If I had to swear as to which one of you boys belonged to me, I—"

Sax hadn't waited to hear the decision.

God, it still had the power to make him sick, even after all these years. With the perspective of age and distance, Sax could see now that Richard had always been able to manipulate the people around him. Except for Sax, who'd been too much like him to be manipulated.

They'd fought over Sax's decision not to follow Richard into the furniture-manufacturing business. They'd clashed again when Richard had tried to force him into getting involved with Susan Chandler, the eldest daughter of one of the Southeast's largest chair manufacturers.

Sax had refused even to meet the girl, who'd been home on a visit from the school she attended in Switzerland.

He'd seen her though, and he still remembered the jolt that had rocked him when he'd looked across the dance floor at that cool, pale face. Probably if Richard hadn't been trying so hard to cram her down his throat, he'd have been on her like a hawk on a rabbit.

Later on he was glad he'd held out. His friend Billy Trent had tried his luck and come away with a bad case of frostbite. According to Billy, she was after richer game then the son of a CPA. Rumor had it during that summer that Susan Chandler wasn't interested in any man whose net worth wasn't well into seven figures.

Sax had seen her several times—usually at the club, with her parents and a skinny kid with braces, glasses and pigtails. She hadn't even bothered to look around at the local talent, most of which was drooling at her from a safe distance.

Sax hadn't drooled. At twenty-three, he'd been extremely suave. Instead, he'd memorized every detail of her appearance, from her polished black hair to her long, slender legs. After all this time, he could still picture her. He'd seen something on the network news a few years ago about Malcolm Chandler's having flown his small plane into a mountain after a scandal that had brought his company, Chandler Chair, down about his ears. Chandler's wife had been killed, too, he recalled.

He wondered how Susan was faring now, without Mal Chandler to keep her in Swiss schools and Italian sports cars. She'd probably found someone else to fill the position by now. Thank God he'd had sense enough to stay clear.

* * *

Gale Chandler Evanshaw stared out at the fog that wisped through the woods toward the house. She'd taken the Limoges tea set to the local antique dealer, Mr. Crump, today. Now she was left to deal with the feelings of guilt that invariably accompanied such transactions.

It did no good to tell herself that it was for Richard; that as the widow of his son, she had some claim to the family heirlooms—even those that had been crammed into a cupboard, some of them chipped, all of them evidently unvalued. The truth was, she hadn't even been married long enough to feel like an Evanshaw. The fact that Jeff had been Richard Evanshaw's adopted son didn't help, either.

She still felt guilty, but what else could she do? Both Olivia and Richard's business manager, Tad Benton, were unavailable. Her sister Susan was in Italy, and Gale had nowhere else to turn. The bank was being downright stuffy about the household account, and Gale had already almost exhausted her personal one. If she'd known Mr. Benton was going to be gone, she might not have encouraged Olivia to go on that cruise.

But of course, Olivia had needed to get away. Losing her only son and, to all intents and purposes, her husband, in the same year, had been a tremendous blow. Gale had been ready to move out and find a place of her own, perhaps in Asheville, when her father-in-law had suffered his stroke. After that, there'd been no question of her going. Olivia had needed her.

The older woman had held up better than Gale had dared expect, even throughout all the endless meetings with Mr. Benton and old Everette Hale, the Evanshaws' lawyer. Drastic changes, it seemed, had been necessary in the family financial arrangements, none of which had involved Gale. Indeed, it never seemed to have occurred to anyone that she had little money of her own, as her father's insurance policies had been declared invalid. She also had no means of producing any after his plane accident unless she sold her photographic equipment. It was the only thing of value she owned.

When she'd finally worked up her nerve to broach the subject with Olivia, she'd been offered a small allowance in exchange for helping manage the house.

Knowing the job would only be for the short period of time until Olivia got back from her cruise, rested and ready to take over, Gale had agreed to the arrangement. Mrs. McCrary, the housekeeper, came three days a week and did as little as possible, and lately Saxon Hall had been showing increasing signs of neglect.

Of course, the 112-year-old mansion was much too large for two women. Before she'd left, Olivia had made an effort to consolidate things so that they could close off all but a few rooms. At the same time she'd sent all the lovely old oriental rugs in the house out to be cleaned. Gale had taken it as a signal that she was beginning to come out of her depression.

Olivia had also stored away much of the unused china and crystal, and for that, Gale was thankful. Mrs. McCrary came late and left early, drinking numerous cups of brandy-laced tea as she rearranged the dust. As the brandy-to-tea ratio increased, she and her feather duster were becoming a real hazard.

Olivia had only been gone for little more than a week when the bills had started pouring in. Until then, Gale had welcomed the privacy, and the chance to get on with her own work without having to defend herself from derisive comments.

She couldn't help but be defensive. The truth was, she'd never really cared for her mother-in-law. Olivia had known that she and Jeff weren't getting along too well, but Gale had seen no point in telling her that she'd asked for a divorce only weeks before Jeff had missed a sharp curve and driven his Ferrari off a cliff coming home from a party with some of his wilder friends.

The darkroom had been her escape, both before and after Jeff's death. She'd ignored Jeff's taunts about her "snapshots" just as she'd shut her ears to Olivia's pointed remarks about hiding out in the basement when she should be starting on a family. Richard had simply ignored the whole matter.

Illustrating children's books with photographs might not be considered serious work by some, but it had been Gale's dream for years. Sometimes it helped enormously just to view the world through a small aperture. For months after her parents had been killed, she hadn't even loaded the film. It had been simply a means of numbing the pain until she could bring her life into focus once more.

Even before they'd gotten back from their honeymoon, Gale had begun to suspect that she'd made a grave mistake. Shortly after their return, she'd dug out her old stories and sketches, the ones she'd begun while she was still in school, and asked permission from Richard to set up her darkroom in an unused corner of his basement.

He'd nodded absently without even looking up from his *Wall Street Journal*. Olivia had lifted a carefully groomed eyebrow and murmured something about smelly chemicals. Jeff had shown his resentment by choosing that moment to announce his plans to fly down to Cozumel with a few friends—male and female—for the diving.

Gale suspected she owed her sanity now to the fact that she could lose herself in her work for long stretches of time. Unfortunately, after months of concentrated effort, her avocation was still just that. She'd accumulated an assortment of stuffed toys, and had created a story around them in which, Golly, a stray mutt, joins forces with Boy, an orphan, in a quest for a home. During their adventures along the way, they meet up with Tripod, the three-legged elephant, and Greselda, a scruffy and extremely pregnant cat, as well as Miss Vanilla, the woman who eventually gives them a home.

Gale had problems including Miss Vanilla in the photographs. She didn't want to use a mannequin, so in the end, she'd resorted to using bits and pieces of the woman in a few shots—a high-topped shoe, the sleeve of a coat with a glove attached—and focused on the toys, instead of the one human character. She'd been greatly encouraged by the favorable response to her proposal, but the publisher refused to go to contract without seeing the completed project, leaving Gale's limited resources to carry it through.

Which meant that in the short time since Olivia had left, Gale had been forced to sell what little jewelry she had, plus several pieces of antique china that didn't belong to her.

It was all an unfortunate mix-up, of course. Olivia had assured her that everything was in order, and that if anything came up before she returned, Gale had only to call on Tad Benton.

Gale had brushed off her reassurances, knowing that Olivia would only be gone a few weeks. What could come up in that length of time? Richard's condition had stabilized and there was no reason to expect any change there.

But then the bills had started arriving. There'd been a statement from Richard's physician and another from the masseuse. The one from the nursing home for a new wool mattress pad and miscellaneous supplies had been stamped overdue. The one from the oil company had been a final notice.

She'd called Tad Benton, and that was when she'd discovered that he was, of all unlikely things, on some sort of nature jaunt in the Galápagos Islands!

Tad Benton, whose wing tips were always flawlessly polished and whose ties and socks were always perfectly matched. She hoped he picked up a miserable case of prickly heat—he deserved it for going off at a time like this and leaving his clients with nothing more than an answering service!

Gale raked her fingers through her dark hair, rumpling it until it stood out about the pale oval of her face. God, she was tired! And worried. Not to mention mad as hell, and a little bit frightened. It was getting so she hated to go to the mailbox, even though she was desperately looking for a letter from Olivia. How was it *possible* for things to get in such a state in two week's time?

Unless one or the other of them checked in soon, things were apt to get a lot worse before they got better. The jewelry had covered the phone company's bill when they'd threatened to cut off service. Now the oil company was refusing to refill the tank until she sent them a check. She couldn't blame them. The balance due sounded more like a national debt than heating service for a modest sixteen-room house.

There was no telling *who* was going to cut off *what* next.

Switching off the lights behind her as a conservation measure, Gale voiced her concerns to the empty house. "The king's out of commission, the queen's out of reach and the comptroller's off chasing turtles!"

Of course, there was one other player—the crown prince. Not that anyone ever mentioned his name in her hearing. There weren't even any pictures of Richard's older son in the home that bore his name, but Gale knew about him. She couldn't help but be curious, especially since she'd married into the Evanshaw family. Like every other female past puberty who'd ever laid eyes on Saxon Evanshaw, she still harbored secret fantasies about the strikingly attractive man with the dark hair and the penetrating blue eyes.

Had Saxon Evanshaw been notified of his father's illness? Or did he just not care? Rumor had it that years ago, while she'd still been away at school, there'd been some sort of fireworks between Richard and his elder son. Saxon had left home, and as far as she knew, he'd never been back.

Three days later, Gale was relaxing in front of a small electric heater rationalizing the sale of a porcelain chocolate pot when the doorbell rang. Her thoughts flew immediately to the dealer who'd bought the tea set, the chocolate pot and several pieces of her personal jewelry. Who else would come all the way out here on a night like this?

He'd changed his mind, she thought, her heart sinking. He wanted his money back. She'd made a point of showing him the broken place inside the lid; it had dropped the value enormously, of course, but it had still brought in enough to replace Richard's tape player.

It was Gale's theory that music might be beneficial for the comatose man, and she'd taken her own tape player out to Laurel Hill Nursing Home for him. Unfortunately, it hadn't been long before it mysteriously "disappeared." She'd raised the devil with the staff, which hadn't helped, and then gone out and bought him another one. She'd also gone to the additional expense of having a lock installed on one of his dresser drawers, with the permission of the nursing-home administrator.

"Look," she said, swinging wide the heavy front door, "if you've changed your mind, I'm sorry, but I've already spent..." Her voice trailed off as she stared up into a lean, deeply tanned face. As though it were a double exposure, Gale saw another image in the half familiar face, the deep-set blue eyes and the windblown gray hair, an image she'd carried for years in some dark corner of her mind without even being aware of it.

"Saxon Evanshaw?" she whispered. Dear Lord, the years certainly hadn't treated him kindly.

Sax took his time. If nothing else, the years had taught him to guard his feelings. She'd already spent *what*, he wondered idly as he studied the woman before him. Susan Chandler? What the devil was she doing here?

Her hair was no longer the polished ebony cap he remembered, but her face hadn't changed all that much. The same dark eyes, widening now, as if she'd seen a ghost. Without lipstick her soft, pale lips looked oddly naked. She was smaller than he remembered, but then, he'd never been this close before. The last time he'd seen Susan Chandler, it had been from across a crowded dance floor. She'd been dressed in something black and expensive, and had looked extremely bored.

Now dressed in a pair of drab corduroys and a baggy black sweatshirt imprinted with a preening flamingo, she looked considerably younger. The fact that she wore a pair of yellow bunny slippers on her feet probably helped.

Slippers? *Here?* "Excuse me for asking, Miss Chandler," Sax said politely, "but what's going on around here?"

"It's Evanshaw," she said in a voice that was barely audible. Still clinging to the door as if it were a life raft, Gale struggled to maintain her composure. "*Mrs.* Evanshaw," she stressed. Dear Lord, did he even know about Jeff? Did he know his father had married Olivia and adopted her son? She'd still been away at school then, and she couldn't remember if that had happened before or after Saxon had left home.

Did he know about Richard?

"May I come inside, Mrs. Evanshaw?" Sax drawled. But even with a cold wind at his back, he was no longer sure he wanted to. Perhaps he'd have done better to book a room at a motel after he'd seen his father, staying clear of this place and all the old memories it held.

Gale managed to tear her gaze away from the rugged face and anchor it somewhere in the vicinity of the heavy brass zipper tab on his leather jacket. How did one greet the prodigal son of a stepfather-in-law? Was it her place to welcome him into his own ancestral home? Who took precedence, the man on the doorstep, or the woman in possession?

"Oh, heavens," Gale murmured, her gaze following the brass teeth of the zipper downward. He was wearing jeans that encased his long, muscular legs, stopping at the insteps of a pair of well-worn Western-style boots. Hardly what she'd have expected of the son of one of the Southeast's oldest, not to mention most prosperous, families.

At this moment, Gale was certain of only one fact: any female past the age of thirteen who'd ever laid eyes on Saxon Evanshaw would've had a hard time forgetting him. She'd only been exposed twice, once when she was thirteen, and again when she was fifteen. She hadn't forgotten either occasion.

"May I come in?" Sax asked again. There was no hint of reprimand in his tone, none of the curiosity he must be feeling at finding a stranger in his home. Instead, he smiled. Almost.

"I'm sorry...you startled me. That is, I wasn't expecting you," Gale exclaimed, gesturing for him to enter. "Please come inside. You probably know how seldom people come this far out. That is, we're so far off the beaten track."

Saxon paused just inside the door, fighting against the sudden onslaught of memories. He thought he'd been prepared for them.

He wasn't.

As his gaze swept the square foyer, with its faded French wallpaper and its aged parquet floors, he inhaled automatically expecting the scent of beeswax and lemon oil. It was there, but it was barely perceptible. The floors were bare, and it was obvious that it had been some time since they'd been buffed. Pale rectangular shapes indicated quite clearly the position of the oriental rugs that had graced the foyer for as long as he could recall.

Under the light of a pewter chandelier, Gale took in details that had been hidden by the darkness outside. The hair she remembered as being thick and dark brown was still just as thick, but there were flecks of gray now, and fine lines at the outer corners of his eyes. He looked as if he spent a good deal of time outdoors.

"Come on into the study, it's warmer there. Would you care for anything? Have you had dinner?" Her mind raced ahead to the barren refrigerator. Dinner for her had been a sandwich, eaten while she pored over proof sheets and mapped out the next day's shooting.

"Thanks. I'm not hungry."

"Have you been—" To visit Richard, she'd been about to say. But if he didn't know about Richard's stroke, she'd need to break the news gently. "Have you been here long?" she finished instead. Questions formed a logjam in her mind. Why had he left home? If he and Richard had fought, what had it been about? Did he know Richard had remarried? Had that been a point of friction between them? Sometimes children resented a parent's remarrying.

"Not long," Sax replied in answer to her hesitant question. He had questions of his own, but he'd finally learned the lesson his father had tried so hard to instill in him. He'd reserve comment until he had all the facts.

After that intensive look when he'd stepped inside, she seemed unable to meet his eyes.

She brushed at her hair to no effect, and then smoothed down the front of her sweatshirt. Saxon couldn't help but question why she was uneasy.

Was he supposed to know why Susan Chandler was here, calling herself Mrs. Evanshaw? To his knowledge, there were no male Evanshaws of marriageable age.

Unless...

"You're *Jeffry Donner's wife*?" Good God, she had to be ten years older than Jeff was—not that she looked it, he'd have to admit.

If anything, she grew paler. Sax saw something of the Susan he remembered as she tilted her chin, exposing a throat that was incredibly graceful. "I'm Jeff's widow," she said quietly, and he sagged into the nearest chair and stared at her.

"His widow? I don't understand."

"No, I don't suppose you do. You left town so long ago, I never even got to meet you." If there was an element of accusation in her words, Sax chose to ignore it. On the verge of probing for more information, he hesitated. Her lips, pink only a moment ago, were almost as pale as her face, and her eyes...

God, how could he have forgotten those eyes? They were the color of smokey topaz—now gray, now amber—and shockingly clear. Jeffry's widow? No wonder she looked like she'd been staked out on top of the mountain. "Uh, is there anything I could get you— like a drink or something?"

"I should be asking you that." Gale uttered a sound that was somewhere between a laugh and an apology. "I'm afraid I'm not a very good hostess." *Stupid,*

Gale—really stupid! You've been here only a few years; Saxon was born here.

"Shall I ring for Hetty?" Sax glanced around and stopped cold. "What happened to the China Trade paintings?"

"Hetty?" Gale repeated.

"The nautical paintings that used to hang in a double row over there. My grandfather bought them from a dealer in Kowloon the year my mother was born."

Gale stared at the pale rectangles on the age-darkened cherry paneling. "Oh. They're on loan. To the art museum in Raleigh. I think it's a traveling exhibition of some sort."

"And the rugs?" he asked softly. "Are those on loan, too?" There wasn't a single one of the fine old orientals he'd grown up with in evidence.

Gale's hand flew to her throat in an instinctively defensive gesture as guilt washed over her. Why was he looking at her this way? Did he think she'd stolen his rugs? Did he know about the things she'd sold?

What if Mr. Crump had put them in his store window? What if Saxon had driven past and recognized his family heirlooms and was trying to trap her into incriminating herself? "The cleaners," she blurted. "They're at the cleaners!"

Thoroughly puzzled at her overreaction, Saxon backed off. "Did I hear you offer a drink? You wouldn't have any coffee made, would you?" *Ease up, Evanshaw! Whatever else she is, the woman's a widow.* And from the looks of her, he mused, a fairly recent one. How the devil could he find out what had happened without making things worse?

"Coffee! I'll make some." Grateful for an excuse to escape, Gale jumped up and hurried to the door.

"Would you care for something to eat? I could make sandwiches."

"Coffee's just fine," Sax assured her.

The moment the door swung closed behind her, he was on his feet, prowling. This room, with its leather upholstered furniture and the walls of books, had been the scene of that last bitter confrontation. It had been here that he'd learned that the man he'd considered his father for twenty-four years might not actually have fathered him, after all. And if he had, there was a distinct possibility that Jeff Donner had been his half brother, as well as his stepbrother.

What relation did that make him to Susan Chandler? Susan Evanshaw, he corrected himself.

Restlessly, Sax moved about the room, touching a well-remembered boulle inkstand, reaching absently for a small bronze that was no longer there. Other things were no longer there, he noted. He reminded himself that it was only natural for a new wife to want to leave her imprint on her home.

That would have been Olivia's doing, probably—the new Mrs. Evanshaw. Now it appeared there was more than one woman bearing that title.

He swore silently, cupping a fist in one hand to keep from pounding the dusty surface of the library table. It was obvious that something was going on around here, something unpleasant. Richard was no longer able to look after his own interests, but someone had to.

"I brought along cheese and rye bread," Gale said as she shouldered her way into the room with a large, plastic tray.

"Let me take that." Sax reached for it, his hands covering hers momentarily, and Gale's eyes met his,

startled by her own reaction to the touch of his warm
flesh.

"It's not heavy," she said breathlessly, raking her
portfolio aside so that he could place it on the low table in front of the sofa.

"Not like the Saxon coffee service, at least."

She laughed. "No, thank goodness. Glass and
plastic don't tarnish, either. Cream and sugar?"

"No thanks. Where's Hetty? Don't tell me she finally retired."

"She must have been before my time. We have Mrs.
McCrary now—when she bothers to show up." Gale
concentrated on pouring without spilling. She was
usually steady as a rock, but for some reason her
hands wouldn't behave tonight.

It was Saxon Evanshaw. He'd brought a disturbing
element into the old house. Along with the scent of
leather, cold air and warm spice that had swept in
through the door with him, there was something less
tangible, but far more real. A feeling of suppressed
energy. A force field that repelled even as it attracted.

"I'm sorry I can't offer you dinner. If I'd known
you were coming, I'd have shopped."

"Don't you usually eat dinner?" She didn't look as
if she ate regularly, but then, maybe she was still
grieving. Or maybe she was just trying to stay fash-
ionably thin. Sax surveyed the slight frame under what
appeared to be layers of clothing. The sweatshirt alone
could have housed a litter of St. Bernard pups.

"I'm not fussy. A sandwich does me just fine."

Sax found that he was hungrier than he'd thought.
He downed two thick cheese, butter and rye sandwiches and helped himself to a second mug of her
coffee. The silence was broken by small homey

sounds—a branch scraping against the eaves, the tick of a clock somewhere in the room.

Unwanted memories drifted back of a small boy driving a Matchbox fleet around the intricate obstacle course of a richly patterned rug, with full sound effects. He shook them off.

Glancing from the cheap electric heater half hidden behind the sofa to the empty tile-faced fireplace, Sax frowned. Why didn't she build a fire or turn up the thermostat instead of bringing in a piece of junk? His father wouldn't have used something like that to heat the kennels, much less his own study.

More than ever, Sax was aware of something just beneath the surface, something that wasn't as it should be. His father had been ill for two months, hardly time enough for things to fall apart.

Where was Olivia? What had happened to her son? It seemed a bit tactless to ask point-blank, but for the life of him he didn't know any other way to find out what he needed to know.

"It's quieter than I remembered," he ventured.

Gale looked up from her lap, where she'd been nursing half a cup of cold coffee. "All the new development went in the other direction. Zoning laws are trying to save what's left of the scenery around here before it all gets bulldozed and paved over."

"Speaking of paving over, what happened to the driveway? Don't tell me the groundhogs have developed a taste for asphalt?"

An amber glint of amusement shafted through Gale's eyes, causing Sax to miss half of her reply. " . . . winter, and then the wet spring."

He gave up. Patience had been hard enough to learn; he'd yet to master subtlety. ''Why don't you tell me where the rest of the family is, Mrs. Evanshaw?''

Chapter Two

Gale chose her words carefully, in case Saxon hadn't yet heard about his father's condition. "At the moment, there's only me. Everyone else is away."

"Away?"

"On a cruise. At least, Olivia is. You do remember Olivia?" she ventured cautiously.

"I remember Olivia," he assured her, his voice expressionless. "My father's wife."

"Yes, well..." Taking a deep breath, she plunged ahead. "After—I mean, her doctor recommended a change, and since there was this cruise available, it, um, seemed like a good idea." Legs crossed at the ankles, elbows close to her sides, Gale held her mug as primly as if she were taking tea with the rector. In an oversized sweatshirt and bunny slippers, the effect was somewhat diminished.

"What about my father?" He'd meant, "How could any wife go off on a cruise and leave a man in that condition?" but evidently he'd been misunderstood.

Gale's fingertips whitened against the stoneware mug. She'd known it was coming, but she still didn't know how to break the news to him. If only she knew him better.

If only he weren't so grim. "Saxon—" She bit her lip. He hadn't invited her to call him by his first name. "Mr. Evanshaw, I'm not sure how to tell you this, but your father's . . . not well."

Saxon's lips thinned as he continued to pin her down with those remarkably expressionless blue eyes of his. They were the color of a January sky, and just about as warm. How could she explain anything to such a man?

"I'm afraid your father suffered a stroke earlier this fall. He's—that is, his condition has stabilized so that he's out of the hospital now. He's at the Laurel Hill Nursing Home." She paused, searching for some clue as to how he was taking the news. "I'm sure if you called, they'd be glad to let you see him."

"Thanks. I already have. I went by there as soon as I got to town."

Gale's mug tipped precariously, and Saxon reached for it and placed it on the orange plastic tray. "You *what*? Then why didn't you say something. Why did you let me stumble around, searching for a way to break the news to you? I thought—I didn't know . . ."

"There's no reason why you should," he replied coolly. "A friend of mine saw fit to drop me a note a few days ago. Decent of him, considering the fact that none of my so-called family bothered to notify me."

"Now wait a minute," she began. She had enough to feel guilty about, but tracking down the black sheep of the family and keeping him posted was not one of her obligations. If Olivia had wanted him to know, she could have gotten in touch with him. Evidently his whereabouts weren't entirely unknown. "I don't know you. I've never even heard your name mentioned in this house. If you knew Richard was ill, why did you wait so long to come home? You should have been here anyway—your father's not a young man anymore."

For one long moment, looking into those accusing eyes, Sax considered telling her precisely why he'd waited even a moment after hearing the news. But if she didn't know about what had happened between him and his father eleven years ago, then she'd never understand why he'd been hesitant.

The truth was he'd been scared stiff that his presence in the same room with the man who'd once called him a bastard—the man he still loved more than anyone on earth—might bring on a serious setback.

He'd stood just inside the door tonight, so damned choked up he could hardly breathe. He'd been so worried about his father's reaction that it hadn't occurred to him he might have problems of his own. It had been all he could do not to gather that frail figure up in his arms and cry like a baby.

Abruptly, Sax stood up and looked around for his coat. "I'd better get out of here," he muttered.

"You're going? Do you have to? I mean, I could make up a room for you upstairs." A few minutes ago, she hadn't wanted him here. Now she didn't want him to go. Gale didn't even attempt to understand her own reactions. "This is your home, after all."

"Is it?" he asked. His eyes were bleak with pain and what appeared to be exhaustion. "It doesn't feel like my home. As a matter of fact, it doesn't even look very much like it."

"There are bound to be changes after all this time. Saxon—Mr. Evanshaw, you're welcome to stay. There's certainly plenty of room."

"Thanks, but I'm booked at Sugar Ridge Inn." It was a lie. He just needed to get out of there so that he could think. Seeing his father had been enough of a shock; now, seeing his old home so cold and barren and unfamiliar was more than he could handle tonight.

Gale followed him from the study, feeling awkward, depressed and oddly angry. She hadn't missed his pointed looks at the bare floors and the bare walls. She opened her mouth to apologize once more and then snapped it shut.

Dammit, what did the man expect? Should they have cast the whole house in bronze as a monument to where he'd once lived?

All right, so maybe tomorrow she'd see if she could track down the name of the rug cleaner and find out how much it was going to cost to get them back. A loan from Fort Knox, probably. But she could hardly call the museum and tell the curator that Mrs. Evanshaw had changed her mind and wanted her paintings back. The exhibit had probably been booked for ages.

She'd do better to worry about paying a few more bills, which meant either going another few rounds with the bank or finding something else to sell.

Either way she ended up feeling frustrated and mad. And just as broke as ever.

"I'll be in touch," Saxon said, turning as he reached the door.

"Fine," Gale said distractedly. She'd practically barreled into him when he'd stopped. Stepping back, she cleared her throat and forced a smile. "Fine," she repeated firmly.

Pieces of the puzzle that made up Saxon Evanshaw continued to haunt her long after he'd gone. She could only conclude that he resented her being there. She couldn't much blame him; it was his home. She'd probably have felt the same way in his place.

Not that she'd ever developed any deep-seated attachment for her parents' home, with its flawlessly manicured grounds and its flawlessly decorated rooms. She'd been away at school from the time she was eight, and few of her vacations had been spent with her parents.

That had been their choice, not hers. Her mother had her committees, her father had his business and his hobby. Malcolm Chandler had raised orchids.

And of course, they both had Susan.

Susan had been born beautiful. She'd never gone through an awkward stage. Gale's awkward stage had lasted until she was almost twenty. Susan had been a top student, whereas Gale had struggled to be adequate. She'd excelled in anything creative, but barely scraped through the rest of her classes.

Malcolm Chandler had sent his favorite daughter off to school in Switzerland to keep her from running off with any of the "wild local bucks." To her father's acute dismay, Susan had promptly fallen in love with the son of an Italian shoe manufacturer.

Gale had gone to boarding school in Connecticut and then come back to North Carolina to attend college. When she'd dropped out in her third year, her parents hadn't even noticed.

Of course, by that time her father had been drowning in a sea of his own problems.

Malcolm Chandler's father had spent years building one of the most successful chair-manufacturing concerns on the East Coast. His son had doubled its size and then proceeded to gut it. The scandal had shaken the whole industry, throwing twelve hundred people out of work and robbing countless more of their retirement benefits. Some had called it suicide when he'd taken off in his plane with his wife during a driving rainstorm and flown into the side of a mountain; Gale had told herself it had been a mistake.

It had all been a mistake. If he'd lived, he'd have straightened it out somehow. She had to believe that.

The accident had happened less than a year after Gale had married Jeff Evanshaw. She knew for a fact that if it had happened before, Jeff would never have married her. Her charming husband had made that fact quite clear; he'd only married her to please Richard, who'd dreamed of combining the two firms into a single giant.

Gale had come home starry-eyed from Susan's wedding in Italy and had promptly been swept off her feet by the handsome Jeff Donner Evanshaw. It had been spring, and several of her school friends had recently been married. When Jeff presented himself at her side at a dance one night, his bright gold hair slightly rumpled, and a tiger lily in the lapel of his dinner jacket instead of the more prosaic rosebud or carnation, she'd been slightly bemused. Before the evening was over, she'd been enchanted.

By the time spring had melted into summer, she'd been thoroughly convinced that they were both head over heels in love. Jeff, in the charmingly outrageous way that was uniquely his own, could make a woman believe almost anything. For a little while, at least. Long enough to get what he wanted.

They'd gone first to tell her parents after eloping to South Carolina. Her father had stared at her, allowing his glasses to slide down his nose, and told her to go find her mother.

Her mother had been counting out invitations to a charity auction. She'd waved a hand for silence and gone on counting, leaving Gale standing in the doorway as if she were a child, waiting to ask if she could go out and play. "I'm married, mother. Jeff and I were married yesterday."

"Thirty-seven, thirty-eight...married, dear? Thirty-nine, forty!" She'd thumped the edges to line them up and dropped them into a box, then reached for another pile. "Why on earth didn't you tell me? We'd have put on a little something right here at home. The roses are perfect now."

Jeff had waited outside. She'd planned to call him in, but it had hardly seemed worth the effort. She'd only have interrupted her mother's counting again.

Olivia had been decidedly cool, and Gale had been intimidated by the flawless blond beauty of a woman whose age she couldn't even begin to guess.

Richard had given her one long, considering look, as if he really saw her as an individual—not as Mal Chandler's little girl or Susan's kid sister, but as a woman in her own right. Very gravely, he'd taken her hand and gripped it firmly. "I hope you'll be very happy," he'd said.

Richard had been the only one to wish them luck. He'd sent for champagne, even though it had only been about two in the afternoon. Jeff had strutted around the study, drinking several glasses and smiling that unbelievably beautiful smile that had caused her to melt the first time she'd seen it.

After that, Richard had reverted to the same gruffness she'd come to expect from her own father. It had been comforting in a way. At least she'd felt more at home.

At the time, she'd been unaware that Richard had once had plans for Saxon and Susan. That knowledge had come later, a part of the process of disillusionment that had started with Jeff's first tantrum.

There was no other word to describe his reactions when Richard had refused to lend him the Saab. Jeff was not the world's greatest driver, and when he'd been around several of his stock-car racing friends, he was worse than usual. On the way back from the Charlotte Speedway, he'd taken a curve too fast and damaged his Ferrari.

Gale hadn't blamed Richard for not giving him the keys to one of the other cars, but she'd been truly frightened by Jeff's reaction. His normally pale complexion had been blotched with angry color, his green eyes blazing. He'd actually screamed.

Boyish charm was one thing. Childishness quite another. Gale had soon discovered that her husband's remarkable good looks and charming manners were a mask for a shocking degree of immaturity.

It had been soon afterward that Jeff had told her why he'd married her. "I couldn't have Susan, she was already married. If she'd come home first so that I could have met her, things might have been different."

Gale had marveled at the ego of the beautiful man-child she'd married so impulsively. Didn't he know that Susan would never even have looked at him? She'd been in love with Tonio since the first time she'd laid eyes on him. Besides, she was eight years older than Jeff.

"Father tried to fix it up before."

Fix what? Before what? She'd wondered, but he hadn't explained and she hadn't dared ask.

"Only that didn't work out," Jeff had continued. Sprawled in a teak and leather campaign chair in his white shorts and rugby shirt with a gin and tonic in his hand, he'd looked like a fashion model. He'd been good at poses. "Sooo...it was up to me. Pity Susan didn't teach you a few things about grooming. D'you have to wear those scruffy jeans? Mother could take you up to New York shopping one weekend—she'd probably even put it on her own account if I asked her to."

Money. That had been another thing she hadn't thought about when she'd come back from Susan's wedding. She'd spent a week surrounded by Tonio's wonderful, wildly emotional family, a week that had culminated in a spectacular wedding at the family's palazzo in Florence. She'd come home in a haze of romantic dreams and Jeff had been waiting.

But romantic dreams wouldn't pay the rent—not that Jeff would've had any need to pay for anything. That lack of responsibility hadn't left much room for self-respect. Or anything else.

It was clear now that Richard had hoped for a match between Saxon and Susan. Had that been what had caused the trouble between them?

Poor Richard. Having met Saxon, Gale was beginning to understand why he and Richard had clashed. No house was large enough for two such dominant males.

The sky was clear and the sun glistened on the rain-washed magnolia leaves when Gale climbed out of bed the next morning. She'd been planning to shoot the hayloft scene today if it had still been raining, which would have meant carrying tons of gear and her bag of props up the hill to Otis Pilky's barn.

Instead, she'd take advantage of the weather to shoot the river scenes—which meant slithering down a muddy embankment with tons of gear and her bag of props.

Before heading for the river, Gale stopped by the bank and deposited the check she'd collected for the chocolate pot into her personal account. Ordinarily, it would have gone into the household account, to which Olivia had arranged for her to have access until she returned from her cruise.

Only the bank seemed to have mislaid Olivia's instructions. The first five checks she'd written on that account had bounced, and she had yet to straighten the matter out. The bank refused to honor her signature on a check, nor would they allow her to transfer any of the funds into her personal account. They wouldn't even tell her how much money was left in the account, not that it would have done her much good.

"Crooks," she grumbled, stalking away from the teller machine as she stuffed the receipt into her purse.

Ever since the day when she'd taken her complaint all the way to the branch manager and listened to his hemming and hawing excuses, she'd conducted as much of her banking as possible by machine. At least the robot didn't make her feel as if she'd come with a gun and a bag, demanding that they "fill 'er up!"

"It's got to be those blasted computers, Mr. Bahanian!" she'd argued. "Are you going to let me starve because a voltage drop wiped out all the bank's assets?"

"Mrs. Evanshaw, I can assure you that, er, um, hmm, and eh . . ."

"Does that mean you're not going to let me use that money?"

"Mrs. Evanshaw, you're perfectly free to use your personal account for as long as you, ah, er, um."

"My personal account, as you damned well know, Mr. Bahanian, is running on fumes!"

"Mrs. Evanshaw, there's no need—"

"And what's all this *Mrs. Evanshaw* business? Mr. Bahanian, you've known my family since before I was born!"

After that gaffe, what could she have said? Of course he'd known her family. If not personally, certainly by reputation. So had everyone else in western North Carolina; everyone in the furniture industry; everyone who ever read a newspaper, listened to the news on radio, television or over the back fence—and certainly every one of the stockholders who'd lost their shirts, thanks to her father's manipulations.

Laurel Hill Nursing Home was a good fifteen miles from Saxon Hall. Normally Gale stopped there first as she was often tired, hungry, and occasionally wet and muddy, too, after a day spent scrambling for the best angles to shoot from. She tried not to allow herself to get discouraged by Richard's continued lack of progress, and it was a lot easier to be cheerful in the morning when she was warm and dry and well fed.

Olivia had found it too depressing to go to the nursing home almost from the first. She claimed it broke her heart to see her husband lying there like a wax effigy. So Gale had taken over the task of paying daily visits to the nursing home. Oddly enough, she found something almost soothing in talking to the man who was her father's contemporary. Not by so much as the flicker of an eyelash did he acknowledge her presence, but at least he didn't walk off in the middle of one of her sentences, as her father used to do. Or worse, turn and start talking to someone else while she was telling him an idea for a new story.

Between Olivia's moodiness and the housekeeper's brandy-laced tea breaks, Gale was glad of any excuse to stay away from the old rock house. Laurel Hill was a haven of peacefulness. Or at least it had been, before the bills had started coming in and she'd begun feeling like a criminal every time she crept past the door of the business office.

Gale heard nothing at all from Saxon that day. She'd hung around until almost eleven in case he called or came by, and then, with a feeling of defiance she hadn't bothered to analyze, she'd thrown her things into her car and headed for the river rather than pay her customary visit to Richard.

Actually, it was only a creek, but as far as her storybook characters were concerned, it was the Mighty French Broad River. She wasn't above taking a few liberties; camera angles could make a world of difference.

Not once did she allow herself to wonder where Saxon was and what he was doing as she set up her props, wiring Golly's ears so that they appeared to be blowing out behind him as he swung across the river on a vine. For all she knew, Saxon could have gone back to wherever he'd been hiding all these years, she told herself as she fitted Boy into the tiny harness of the hang glider that would enable him to pluck Golly from the brink of disaster.

She worked until her feet were numb—sneakers probably hadn't been the wisest choice of footwear for today's site. The sandwich she'd brought along was forgotten until late in the afternoon. By then, it was hard and dry, but she ate it anyway, licking the pimento cheese from her cold fingers.

Often during her visits she talked to Richard about her work. She could hardly just sit there for an hour and then leave without saying anything. Today if she'd gone to see him she'd have told him how red the sourwood was, and about the hawk she'd seen circling over a clearing.

She'd have played him some music and then left, promising to come back tomorrow. For reasons she didn't bother to examine too closely, she didn't care to run into Saxon at Laurel Hill. If Emma Matlock, the business administrator, should choose to bring up the subject of the overdue bills with him, she'd be forced to explain what was happening, and how could she, when she didn't understand it herself?

Instead she'd called the home, and was told that Mr. Evanshaw had had a visitor who had stayed most of the day and left only a few minutes ago.

Gale could well imagine the excitement among the younger nurses at the home. The older ones, too, for that matter. Was any woman immune to a man like Saxon Evanshaw? Goodness knows, she wasn't, and she had more reason than most to be wary.

The following morning she selected a Wedgwood compote, a Sunderland sugar bowl and a silver luster pitcher—all odd pieces. Old, but not outstandingly pretty, they'd been packed away in a box and stored in the basement. There were barrels full of china and crystal in the storeroom, all unused as far as Gale could tell. Generations of Saxon and Evanshaw brides had evidently produced an embarrassment of riches.

She hated to touch any of it. If she hadn't eloped so hastily, perhaps she'd have had wedding gifts herself, and wouldn't have had to dip into those that didn't belong to her.

But the nursing home bill couldn't wait. She was sure the sale of the odd pieces wouldn't cover it entirely, but at least it would tide her over.

Surely Olivia or Mr. Benton would be back before too much longer.

Mr. Crump, on Fairview Street, dealt in antiques, collectibles and estate jewelry. He greeted her courteously, as usual, and as usual, Gale felt like a criminal as she let herself into his cluttered little shop. Did he have to have that jangling bell on the door to alert everyone in town that Gale Chandler Evanshaw was back with another "consignment"?

She remembered when places like this were called pawnshops. No one she'd ever known had ever been inside one—or at least admitted it. That was left to the people her mother had called, "Not our sort of folks."

Well, now Gale Chandler Evanshaw was "not our sort of folks." What made it even worse was that the things she traded for cash for the most part didn't even belong to her.

Ten minutes later, she stuffed a check into her purse and hurried around the corner to where she'd left her car. She never parked it in front of Crump's—not that her situation was any secret. Not with the mailman delivering all those windowed envelopes.

In a thoroughly foul mood, Gale stalked along the cracked sidewalk, nodding with grim cheerfulness to everyone she passed and imagining she could hear their whispers as they hurried on about their business.

God, how she hated living in a town where everybody knew her whole life history! Anywhere else in the world, she'd have had her own identity. Only in Shepparton was a woman automatically identified by her family relationships.

It wasn't so much that she was ashamed of her father, or even of Jeff. Neither one of them had ever let her get close enough to feel a sense of responsibility for who they were and what they did. But now that they were gone, why couldn't she be simply Gale—writer and photographer—with a promising future ahead of her?

Instead she was either Miss Chandler, daughter of the man who bilked all those poor people out of their life savings, or Mrs. Evanshaw, widow of that wild Donner boy Richard Evanshaw had adopted—the one who kept getting in trouble until he'd finally gotten drunk one night and driven that fancy car of his right off the mountain.

"Mrs. Evanshaw?"

Gale dropped her purse. Before she could pick it up again, Saxon was handing it to her, his fingers brushing hers with a crackle of electricity that must have dimmed every light between Shepparton and Asheville.

"I thought you'd left town," she said breathlessly.

"Did you?" *Or did you just hope I had?* Sax asked silently. He'd done some checking. The curator of Raleigh's Museum of Fine Arts had never heard of the Evanshaws' collection of China Trade paintings, nor were any of the rug cleaners who specialized in valuable orientals holding any rugs for Mrs. Evanshaw.

If he'd had any remaining doubts about just who was gradually bleeding the estate of its valuables, the look of guilt on Susan Chandler Evanshaw's face would have erased them. "May I buy you a cup of coffee, or are you on your way somewhere?" he asked politely.

"I'm—no. That is, nowhere special."

"Then shall we stop at the Copper Kettle?" He indicated the comfortable run-down place across the street that specialized in country ham, chicken-fried steak and homemade desserts. And Gale, as if she had no more will than one of her stuffed-toy characters, followed obediently.

Sax ordered coffee and a steak biscuit. "I haven't had breakfast," he explained. "Sure you won't have something besides coffee?"

Gale shook her head. Now that she was here, she wondered if she'd taken leave of her senses. Passing the time of day with Saxon Evanshaw was about as safe as waltzing through a mine field. At this moment, she carried in her purse another check from

Elias Crump, along with a receipt for three items that had probably been in Saxon's family for generations.

Gale had grown up with "family things"—Great-aunt Moselle's tea cups, Grandmama Gilbert's berry set. You took them for granted, simply because they'd always been there. That is, you did until one day you looked around and they were missing.

"No thank you," she said primly. "I had breakfast earlier."

It seemed as if that polite exchange had exhausted all avenues of conversation. Saxon glanced around him as if searching for a familiar face among the straggling diners. They were mostly retired people, living on fixed incomes. The Copper Kettle had a reputation for good, plain food for good, plain prices.

Gale stared at the faded café curtains and thought of the faded rectangles on the paneling in the study. Surely he hadn't minded Olivia's having lent the collection to the museum?

She heard the cashier greet a regular by name and make some small joke about saving him the last serving of peach cobbler, and it occurred to her there were advantages to living in a small town after all, as well as disadvantages.

"Coffee's fresh," said the waitress, who eyed Saxon with open appreciation as she poured both cups. "Sure you wouldn't like some home fries? How 'bout a plate of biscuits and redeye gravy? Gale, can I tempt you with some persimmon pudding? Edna saved the last piece of peach cobbler for Mr. Cartwright."

Saxon shook his head, his attention not on the waitress, but on the woman seated across the yellow Formica table from him. Gale? Was that a nickname? He wouldn't have thought the Susan Chandler he remembered would be on such friendly terms with someone who waited tables in a cheap café.

"Gale?" he inquired as soon as they were left alone.

"Yes?"

"She called you Gale. I thought your name was Susan." His tone was suspicious, almost accusing, and Gale sighed, wondering what else could happen to complicate an already complex situation.

Chapter Three

Saxon watched until Gale turned the corner at Main and McDowell Streets and disappeared behind the First Baptist Church.

Gale Chandler. Not Susan, but *Gale*!

No wonder she'd stuck in his mind like a burr ever since he'd seen her standing there in the doorway, her slight body swallowed up by that monstrous sweatshirt she'd been wearing, and her pale features eclipsed by those remarkable eyes of hers. The coloring was the same, as was the basic bone structure—the angle of the cheekbones, the height of the forehead. There was definitely a resemblance, all right, but Gale barely reached the top button of his shirt. She was obviously younger, too, now that he was aware of it, with none of the hard polish that had kept him from even wanting to get close to her sister.

He should have been more observant—perhaps he would have been if he hadn't just come from seeing his father. The changes that had taken place in the older man in the years since he'd last seen him had been almost too much for Saxon.

So this was Gale Chandler. She must have been that scrap of a kid in braces, glasses and pigtails he'd seen from across the club dining room that day with Susan and Malcolm Chandler. Richard had started in on him right after that.

"It wouldn't have hurt you just to walk across the room and *meet* the girl!" Richard had roared that night so long ago. He'd always yelled when his plans were thwarted, as if decibels alone could tip the balance.

"Dad, I told you, I already have a date for the dance."

"I'm not talking about the dance now, I'm talking about my son's not having the common decency to pay his respects to the daughter of one of my dearest friends. Susan just got home for the holidays. She doesn't know a soul around town anymore, and if you weren't so damned stubborn, you might find out she's just the sort of woman you need!"

"One of your dearest *friends*!" Sax had roared back. "Since when have you and Mal Chandler been friends? A month ago you accused him of polluting the river with waste from his finishing plant, and trying to blame you. Now you want me to marry his daughter?"

"Who said anything about marrying? All I asked you to do was call around there and introduce yourself, offer to show her around."

"If you're so hot on buttering up to Chandler, you do it! I've seen enough to know that she's not my type. Personally, I prefer a woman who runs on blood instead of antifreeze."

"We all know the type of woman you prefer—any floozy you can buy with a couple of drinks is your type. Just once, as a special favor to me, would you make an effort to act like the gentleman you were brought up to be instead of a damned rutting bull moose?"

"Oh, I see now," Sax had said softly. "You want me to choose my friends according to their social and financial standing instead of their—"

"Cup size? You're damned right, boy!"

Sax smiled a little sadly now as he turned toward where he'd parked his rental car. It had been a stupid argument, as all their other arguments had been, only he hadn't been able to see it then. As usual, it had been left to his mother to break it up. Julie Saxon Evanshaw had poked her head through the study door to tell them they were rattling the prisms off the dining-room chandelier, and asked if they'd mind taking their discussion out to the barn where it belonged.

Now, glancing around Shepparton's two-block commercial district—a mixture of the garish new and the faded obsolete, both overshadowed by the magnificent mountains rising on all sides—Sax knew a feeling of overwhelming exhaustion. He'd aged far more than the eleven years that had passed since the night he'd stormed off, driven himself to Norfolk, Virginia, and enlisted in the coast guard. He'd gone too far and stayed away too long.

Maybe it was too late to come home. There was nothing he could do for his father, and as for what was happening at Saxon Hall, why should he care if they cleaned the place out? His father had made his choice clear when he'd married Olivia and adopted her son.

Sax found it bitterly amusing to think that the old guy still hadn't given up playing Cupid. It must have given him quite a thrill to be able to arrange a merger between the Chandlers and Evanshaws after all. Evidently it hadn't provided him with the one thing he'd wanted most of all, though. Jeff must have died before he could produce any grandchildren.

How long had they been married? When and how had Jeff died? Was that the reason things were disappearing from the house now—Gale was afraid that once her mother-in-law got back, she'd be out on her ear?

In a way, he could almost feel sorry for her. She was young to have been left a widow. The puzzling thing was that she continued to stick around that dusty old mausoleum by herself. It couldn't be much fun being stuck out there all alone six miles away from even the small amenities Shepparton had to offer.

Unless she figured that with Olivia gone and Richard out of the picture, she had a perfect opportunity to set herself up for the future. What was it they'd said about Susan? That she wouldn't even look at a man whose income didn't run to seven figures?

Evidently, Gale took after her sister in more than just looks. And since Jeff had died before he could inherit from Richard, she probably suspected that Olivia wouldn't be inclined to be generous.

Sax drove himself out to the interstate and headed for Sugar Ridge Inn, where he'd spent the night. At this point, he wasn't sure of his next step—he needed some answers, and he didn't know where to go to find them. He'd tried to call Billy Trent and missed him.

What puzzled him most was how Gale thought she could get away with it. Hell, a woman like Olivia wouldn't hesitate to bear down hard on anyone who horned in on her territory, daughter-in-law or not. And there was Tad Benton. He should have kept up with things better than this.

Sax pulled into the parking space nearest his room and sat for a moment, his eyes on the blue haze of mountains showing between the row of tall Douglas firs. Concentrating on how best to deal with the situation he'd uncovered at home, he was blind to the magnificent Blue Ridge scenery he'd missed so much for so many years.

Gradually he smiled. It was the sort of smile that would have caused a cautious poker player to fold on two pairs. Climbing out of the car, he strode in the direction of the front office.

Gale gave up all thought of getting any work done. Instead, she stopped by the bank, filled out a deposit slip and handed it over with the check she'd been carrying around in her purse, waiting impatiently while the teller stamped the slip and handed her copy across the high ledge.

"Can I write a check against it now?" She no longer took anything for granted.

"It oughta clear by Monday, Miz Evanshaw. You should be able to write a check against it early next week," the teller replied.

"Next week! I need to write one today! You have your money, why can't I get mine?"

"It takes time for a check to clear, Miz Evanshaw."

"But it's written on this bank!"

"We have to follow procedure, Miz—"

"I don't care about your procedure. It's archaic! It's worse than that, it's criminal!" She hadn't needed this. Frustration had become a way of life for her lately, and she didn't know how much more she could take. If she were being tested, she only hoped the ultimate rewards would be worth it.

"Then just cash it for me," she ordered. She'd pay the bills with cash, which meant paying each one in person. She certainly didn't look forward to that.

"I'm sorry, but I can't do that, Miz Evanshaw. It's already been deposited."

"What do you mean, it's already been deposited? I withdraw my deposit, and don't tell me I can't do that—it's lying right there in front of you. Just give it back to me and—"

"If you'll wait, I'll speak to Mr. Bahanian, but I'm pretty sure we can't do that. The procedure—"

Everyone in the bank was staring at her. Gale could practically read their thoughts: *Malcolm Chandler's daughter. The acorn doesn't fall far from the tree, does it?*

"Never mind," she said through tightly clenched jaws. Crumpling the receipt in her fist, she swung past the security guard, muttering maledictions under her breath.

The guard stared after her, a look of reproach on his ruddy face. Who would have thought a nice young lady like Miss Gale would be using language like that?

Twenty minutes later, Gale handed Emma Matlock at Laurel Hill a postdated check, promising the balance as soon as Mr. Benton or Mrs. Evanshaw returned.

Taking several deep breaths, she made a conscious effort to still her emotions before entering Richard's room. Regardless of what anyone said, she was certain he was aware of her presence, even though he was unable to respond. She was equally sure that even though he lacked the ability to communicate—or possibly even *because* of that fact—he would be affected by her emotions.

She stayed less than an hour today, in case Saxon should choose to visit his father again. She wasn't ready to see him again, not just yet. The man packed a wallop, intentionally or not.

It would hardly be intentional, she reminded herself. They'd only just met, and not under the most promising circumstances, at that. She hadn't bothered to change clothes that day after clambering about the countryside. What a marvelous first impression she must have made!

Today's impression couldn't have been much better. She'd put on her oldest pair of corduroys and a comfortable sweater left over from her college days, planning to explore the orchard she'd discovered after stopping by at Crump's and the bank.

A nurse peered in the door, smiled, nodded and disappeared again. Gale recognized her as one of the private-duty nurses they'd hired for Richard until they were certain the care at Laurel Hill would be adequate.

It was more than adequate, it was excellent. It was also exceedingly costly, and things like the fleecy wool mattress pad and the twice-daily passive exercises by the physical therapist were extra.

"I think I like your older son, Richard," she murmured. She always talked—sometimes just about the weather, or the nest of flying squirrels that had taken over one of the bluebird boxes. "He's more like you than I'd remembered. Or maybe it's the gray hair. It's mostly just on top—still pretty dark around the edges. It's quite striking." She sighed unconsciously. "Next time he visits, open your eyes just a tiny bit and take a peek."

She went on to tell him about an upcoming concert by the coast guard band at the high school auditorium. A true Aries, Richard loved marching music. She'd barged in on him once in his study shortly after she and Jeff had been married. He'd been watching a rerun of *Victory At Sea* on television, and while she'd waited for him to switch it off so that she could ask whatever it was she'd sought him out to ask, he'd started talking about his experiences as a coxswain in the coast guard, landing troops under fire on a Guadalcanal beachhead in World War II.

She'd never looked at him in quite the same way afterward, although he'd quickly reverted to the taciturn retired businessman she was used to.

Now, gazing at the comatose man lying so still on the adjustable bed—asleep, yet not asleep—she thought of the tragedy of having a lifetime of experiences locked away inside a frail body and a mind that was no longer able to reach out. Was he living in the past? Was he aware of what was going on in the present?

Would anyone ever know?

Later that afternoon as she was on the way home, Gale's thoughts drifted inevitably back to Saxon. The truth was, he'd scarcely been out of them since he'd turned up so unexpectedly on her doorstep. Surprised when he'd insisted on staying at a motel, she'd felt compelled to issue another invitation. He'd probably been thinking about the proprieties—a man and woman alone in the house—but that was absurd. This was the eighties, and they were practically kin. She was his . . .

What? His sister-in-law? His stepsister-in-law? His adopted stepsister-in-law?

Oh, what difference did it make? Saxon Hall was his own home, after all. He had far more claim to it than she ever would. Given the choice, Gale would cheerfully have traded her share of the sixteen-room mansion for a two-room apartment of her own choosing.

The phone was ringing when she let herself inside, and she glanced at it warily as she slung her shoulder bag onto a chair. The good news was that it was working—the phone company hadn't seen fit to cut her off yet.

The bad news was that it was probably another creditor. Or the bank, telling her that the check she'd just deposited wasn't good.

It was Saxon. Gale felt her palms grow damp as she gripped the instrument and hooked a chair with one foot so that she could sit down. Funny, she hadn't noticed his voice before—the depth of it, that huskiness that made him sound almost gruff. She'd been too busy noticing everything else about the man.

"Is that invitation still open?" he asked without a preamble.

"Invitation? You mean—here?"

"You said you wouldn't mind if I moved in for a few days. This place is too noisy. I think they were having a party last night in the next unit."

"Well, sure... I mean, you're perfectly welcome. There's certainly plenty of room, and I can guarantee that it's quiet."

It was settled before Gale quite realized what it would mean. She hung up the phone and sat there for several minutes, gazing absently at the shaft of golden light that streamed in through the windows to spill across the bare floor. The windows needed washing. The floors needed waxing, too, before the rugs were put down again.

It was all she could do to dust behind Mrs. McCrary and keep the leaves from banking up on the porch and blocking the front door.

It would've been easier to do everything from scratch herself, instead of trying to work under and around someone else. But since she wasn't in a hiring or firing position, she did the best she could do. Sooner or later, Olivia was going to have to get cracking again. Lately she hadn't even seemed to care about keeping up appearances.

Meanwhile there'd be someone else to worry about. Would Saxon expect someone to cook his meals and look after his room? He probably had no idea how many things had changed around here since he'd been gone. Considering the way things had changed just since Richard had taken ill, it was a wonder he'd even recognized the place.

Oh, he'd spotted the missing rugs and paintings right away. There wasn't much she could do about those at the moment, but maybe she could find the money to hire someone to come in and help her wax the floors and wash all the windows.

And maybe she'd trip over a five-pound emerald while she was out shooting tomorrow and all her problems would be miraculously solved.

Suddenly her thoughts came back to Mrs. Mc-Crary. "Oh, Lord," Gale groaned as she headed for the kitchen to check out the pantry and freezer. She'd have to explain about the housekeeper before Saxon was exposed to the woman. Maybe he'd been too nearsighted to notice the dust she missed and a few smudges here and there.

She'd better call and see if the oil people could be coerced into refilling the tank so that she could turn up the furnace. She'd managed to convince herself that sixty-five degrees was a lot healthier than the seventy-two Olivia preferred, but Saxon might have other ideas.

For the hundredth time since her mother-in-law had left, Gale wondered just how things could have become so snarled up in such a short time. It wasn't anything she'd done—she hadn't *done* anything.

"I think I've covered it all," Olivia had said distractedly as she'd waited beside mounds of luggage for the cab that would take her to the airport near Asheville. "There might be a few loose ends, but I've arranged for you to have access to the household account, and you can always call on Tad Benton." One of the loose ends, it turned out, was that the household account was *not* accessible. Another loose end was that neither was Tad Benton!

The refrigerator looked like one in an unfurnished apartment for rent, and the pantry wasn't much better. Gale raced upstairs and opened the door to one of the nicer bedrooms with a southern exposure. It felt damp and stale. Snatching off the dust covers, she balled them up and tossed them into the hall, plumped the pillows and propped them up, and then threw open both windows to allow the brisk November breeze to blow through.

Then, mentally composing a shopping list and checking it against her meager funds, she headed back to town.

There was a strange car in the driveway when she returned some forty-five minutes later. Pulling up beside it, Gale gathered up three brown paper sacks and her shoulder bag, fumbling for the house key as she hurried to the door.

She hoped for the sake of her budget that Saxon's appetite was moderate. Unfortunately, he struck her as a man without a moderate bone in his body.

"Anybody home?" she called out, slamming the heavy door behind her. She'd never quite grown used to the hollow sound of her own voice in the large, high-ceilinged rooms since the rugs had been taken up. Sometimes she talked to herself just to hear it. Sometimes she sang. But not often. It would take far better acoustics than those of Saxon Hall to make up for her off-key efforts.

"What the hell happened up here? Are you planning on having a white sale?"

"A white sale?" Gale echoed blankly. She was squeezing the whole wheat bread and pushing a can of sockeye salmon perilously close to the top of the sack as she stared up at the man leaning over the banisters. "Oh—the dust covers."

"Speaking of dust—" Sax continued as he came down the wide, curving stairs.

In fascination, Gale watched the subtle flexing of his muscular body as he descended. "I suppose I'd better explain about Mrs. McCrary, Saxon,'' she said, venturing the beginnings of a smile. If they were going to be living here together for the next few days, they may as well get on friendly terms.

She could do with a friend about now, although under the circumstances, Saxon might not be the wisest choice. "She comes three days a week, usually. But sometimes she doesn't get here until close to noon, and then she has to leave before it gets dark, because she doesn't like to drive at night, so—"

"So she come for lunch and what—a snooze?"

Shifting her groceries, Gale grinned. "Tea. Actually, tea and brandy."

"And you still keep her on?" Without asking, he lifted the sacks of groceries from Gale's arms and strode toward the kitchen, leaving her to follow or not.

She followed. "You have to understand, finding someone willing to come all the way out here isn't that easy. Shepparton doesn't have much of a work force these days." Especially not for the amount Olivia was willing to pay—which was twice what Mrs. McCrary was worth, and a good deal more than Gale could afford at the moment.

"How'd you get in?" Gale asked, shedding a layer of sweater and rolling up the sleeves of the one beneath it.

"The key under the edge of the porch. Didn't you know about it?"

Gale shook her head as she ran water in one side of the massive old porcelain sink and dropped lettuce, bell peppers and mushrooms in all at once.

"Good thing the locks haven't been changed—I'd have had to go through the bathroom window."

"The *what*?"

To her delight, Saxon related a few escapades from his past as they washed vegetables and put away the groceries together. Then he asked for the keys to the Jeep. "I'd like to use it while I'm here and turn in the rental car, that is if you have no objections?"

There was nothing overt in his tone of voice, yet Gale was conscious of having been issued some sort of challenge. "Use anything you want to. There are three cars besides mine. The keys are hanging by the utility-room door, but I doubt if the Jeep'll start. No one's driven it since—I mean, it's been several months—"

"Since my father's stroke. You don't have to spare my feelings, Gale. I know my father's in serious shape, and I know I should have come home before now."

Ragged patches of color bloomed in her cheeks. "I didn't mean—I wasn't trying to—"

"Forget it. If we're going to live here together, we may as well clear the air. There are some things you should know—" He broke off, frowning. "But not now. First I want to get my bearings. Eleven years is a long time, and I'm beginning to feel a little like an illegal alien."

Sax unhooked the keys from the shield-shaped board and let himself out the back door without waiting for her response. He knew she was staring after him; he could feel her eyes burning into his back.

It was those eyes of hers that got to him, he decided, as he nosed the rented Ford inside the garage and hunted down a set of jumper cables. No thief should have eyes that clear. They lured a man too close for safety.

As a boy, Sax had never been able to resist exploring the deepest pools, especially those that were so clear he could catch glimpses of sunlight reflected

from the rocks on the bottom. Even the commonest
pebbles turned into gold and gemstones under such
deceptively clear depths.

Inside, Gale heard the Jeep crank up, and then the
slam of two hoods. She let out her breath in one long,
heartfelt sigh. Thank goodness the thing had started.
The sooner he left and the longer he stayed away, the
better she'd like it. Saxon Evanshaw at full maturity
was even more devastating than he'd been in his early
twenties.

It was difficult not to compare Richard's two sons.
Poor Jeff had been little more than a petulant child.
His trying to live up to Saxon would have been rather
like her trying to live up to Susan. After awhile, she'd
given up trying and begun to plot her own course.

And at the moment, she warned herself, she'd better take care where that course led her. She was in
enough trouble without running afoul of another male
Evanshaw.

The first few days went surprisingly well. Gale
didn't mind cooking, especially as Saxon offered to
buy the food if she'd prepare it. Cooking was a relatively new skill for her, and she still tended to be rather
erratic. She gave him fair warning that first night,
when he came in just before dark, smelling of evergreens and cold, damp air.

"The one thing I'm *not*—as a cook, that is—is
mediocre. Either I'm very good, or very bad. If it's
any comfort to you," she offered with a grin, "the
odds lately have been running in my favor."

Since then, she'd scored with a small rib roast, pan-
fried mountain trout, and a ham and cheese casse-
role. Her chicken and apple omelet had been so bad

she hadn't even had the heart to apologize. She'd scraped it out the back door in silent misery for any animal who cared to try his luck. Saxon hadn't said a word, which had only made it worse.

Nor had he complained about his room. Evidently the extra blankets she'd piled on the chest at the foot of the bed had been sufficient. If he'd mentioned the lack of heat, she'd planned to tell him she was waiting for the furnace to have its annual checkup before turning it on.

Evidently he'd forgotten whatever it was he'd wanted to talk to her about that first night, unless it had to do with whether or not he was going to be in for dinner, and how his father was progressing. As for where he disappeared to each day and what he did with all his time, he didn't mention it, and Gale didn't ask.

Which was just as well. She might have been called on to answer a few questions in return, and she'd just as soon not. Gale had suffered her parents' indifference toward her ambitions, her husband's ridicule and her mother-in-law's condescending amusement. Even Richard had evinced no real interest in her work, although he'd been too much of a gentleman to demean her efforts.

Susan had been the only one ever to offer support and encouragement. Gale could have used a generous serving of each about now, but of course Susan was in Italy, and she'd never been much of a correspondent.

Meanwhile, Gale had learned to accept the fact that the only safe time for a writer to come out of the closet was when she had a contract in hand. Or better yet, a published work. Until then, it was easier to go her own way and say nothing.

At least the house no longer seemed so empty. It was surprising what a difference it made to know that someone else slept under the same roof. Gale's room was on the first floor, in a wing of the house that had been supposed to offer a degree of privacy to a newly married couple.

She'd kept the same room, even after the accident. There were no ghosts there—nothing at all of Jeff to haunt her. It was as though he'd been a meteor, burning brightly for a few moments in the night sky, and then disappearing without a trace. There'd been no time to fix a lasting image on her soul, and for that she was grateful.

But there were times when the night was frighteningly dark. There were a trillion stars glowing out there, not one of them seemed able to warm away the coldness that sometimes crept in despite all she could do.

Inevitably, Gale found herself growing more and more curious about the split between Saxon and his father. Living in the same house, it was impossible not to wonder what had gone wrong between them. Richard had been a quiet man, but it was the quietness of great strength, the sort that made even the people who knew him best walk on tiptoe. In Saxon she felt the same sort of leashed energy, as if his emotions ran so deep and so strong that he was on guard every minute to keep from losing control.

Imagine two such men under the same roof!

Was there a way she could help bring them together again, even without knowing what had caused the split? What would the effect be on Richard? She felt almost certain that a reconciliation would have a beneficial effect, but there was still that tiny element of doubt.

She didn't know for a fact that he'd even seen his father since the first few days. If he had, there was the possibility that he'd merely hovered in the doorway. Why did so many people—people like Olivia—think that just because a man was unable to move or speak, he was unaware of what went on around him?

She really needed to talk with Saxon about his father. She just didn't know quite how to bring it up. For two people who were living together and sharing most meals, they were still on remarkably impersonal terms, like boarders at the same boarding house.

Boarders sharing the same last name?

All right, this is it, Gale promised herself as she put the dishes into the dishwasher and made herself a peanut butter and bacon sandwich to take out with her. Tonight she'd tackle him with the subject of how they could best promote Richard's recovery.

And if, in the course of the discussion, Sax should happen to find out that she was barely managing to stay afloat with all the bills that someone had evidently forgotten to pay, then that was all right, too. She'd just as soon end her criminal career before it went much further.

First things first. At the moment the sun was shining, and she had a full day's shooting planned. The creek, possibly the orchard, and Otis Pilky's farm, in that order. Which would take her right past her favorite barbecue place on the way home. After the chicken and apple debacle, she hadn't worked up enough courage to try her hand at cooking again.

Then, thoroughly sated with Punk's Pork Barbecue, and with a fresh pot of coffee brewing, they'd get down to a few brass tacks.

Chapter Four

Sax leaned back in his father's comfortable desk chair while he waited for the banker's secretary to put through his call, and stared at the stacks of bills he'd unearthed.

Unearthed was perhaps too strong a word; they hadn't actually been hidden. But neither had Mrs. Gale Evanshaw been particularly forthcoming about the state of the family finances. With good reason, it seemed. Things were in a mess around here, and it hadn't happened overnight. Evidently, there was a lot more going on than he'd first thought, in which case, that little lady was going to have a lot to answer for when he finally pinned her down.

But first he intended to collect a few more hard facts.

"Bahanian? That's right, Sax Evanshaw. You opened a savings account for me your first day at the bank, remember? I came in with about ten pounds of pennies...." Sax allowed the man his own reminiscences as he toyed idly with the desk pen. A series of linked ovals spread across the top of a sheet of notepaper under his fist.

"Mrs. Evanshaw?" His eyes lost the faintly bored expression. "Hmm, was that Gale Evanshaw or Olivia? Oh. Yes, I see. Must have been an oversight—no, nothing to worry about. Perfectly understandable . . . yes, I'll tell her."

After thanking the branch manager for his time, Sax hung up the phone, scowling thoughtfully at the chain he'd drawn across the top of the page. An oversight, they'd agreed, but had it been an honest oversight? According to the branch manager, Gale had written five checks on an account that was not her own, and when the bank had called her on it, she'd professed innocence. She'd claimed she'd signed some sort of card Olivia had picked up at the bank, which was supposed to have given her access to one of Olivia's and Richard's joint accounts.

She should have known she couldn't get away with it, no matter how illegible her signature was. It would have been simpler when she'd been caught, not to mention much more graceful, to say she'd just picked up the wrong checkbook by mistake.

After a few minutes, Sax reached for the phone, dialed a number and asked for Billy Trent.

Billy was one of the few thirty-five-year-old men he knew who could get away with being called "Billy." "William" simply didn't do justice to the chubby professional good ole boy who probably sold more insurance than any other agent in the state.

"Billy? Sax Evanshaw here. Yeah, I got in a few days ago. Your secretary said you were down in Georgia giving a seminar on actuarial hell-raising."

For the first time since he'd boarded a 737 in Amarillo and headed east, Sax threw back his head and laughed aloud. After listening to a rather lengthy comparison between the Atlanta convention and one of the more notorious events of their prep school days, he chuckled. "Yeah, sounds familiar, all right. I reckon we both pushed the parameters about as far as they'd stretch in those days."

Finally, he took a deep breath. "Billy, tell me what you know about Gale Chandler. Gale Evanshaw, I guess she is now, although damned if I can get used to it."

Gradually, as he listened to the voice on the other end, the laughter faded from Sax's eyes. He swore softly once or twice, and after several minutes he said, "Yeah, sure, Billy. We'll have to get together one day soon and catch up. Meanwhile, thanks a lot, friend. Your annual notes left a lot to be desired when it comes to keeping me abreast of what's going on."

For a long time after he hung up the phone, he simply sat there, staring at the pale rectangles on the dark paneling. And then he swore again.

There was a single light showing in the house when Gale nosed her mustard-colored sedan up to the door of the garage. She'd always parked outside. The garage had been filled to capacity ever since she'd been a member of the Evanshaw family, and it had never occurred to her to ask anyone to move over and make room for her plebeian vehicle.

Gale had been given money for the wheels of her choice when she'd graduated from Miss Winthrop's Boarding School in Connecticut. After one last wistful look at a racy little model she'd long coveted, she'd bought herself a complete set of top-of-the-line darkroom equipment and then visited a local used-car dealer. After much deliberation, she'd settled for a midsized, midpriced four-year-old sedan whose only problem was that it was a rather hideous color, vinyl top and all. It had never given her a moment's trouble, and she comforted herself with the fact that it was easy to find, even in the largest parking lot.

Now, slinging her camera case over her shoulder, she grabbed her bag of props from the back seat and balanced the two Styrofoam barbecue plates under her chin as she let herself in the back door. Just this once she'd like to make it to the kitchen table without dribbling sauce down her coat.

The kitchen light came on suddenly, nearly blinding her. "Oh, hi—glad you're home. I brought supper, and it's still hot."

Sax silently watched her from the doorway.

Gale eased the heavy camera case down onto the counter. She'd dropped the Hefty bag inside the utility room when she'd come through there. "I hope you like ribs," she said brightly, glancing up and then hastily averting her face.

Didn't the man have any idea what he looked like in those jeans? They had to be government issue—coast guard or navy. They fit like a well-worn glove, and there was no fancy stitching to distract the eye from the essential masculinity of the wearer. With that exotic, sable and silver hair of his, a pair of plain Western boots and a navy flannel shirt, Saxon Evanshaw was enough to addle the wits of the most levelheaded of women.

Gale was hardly that at the best of times. From the first moment she's seen him, she'd been struck by an odd sense of recognition. It probably had something to do with that old crush she'd harbored, but it was more than that. There was a strength about Saxon Evanshaw that drew her like a magnet. That strength, added to an inherent sexuality, was a potent force to be dealt with in such close quarters.

"Shall I make coffee?" Sax asked finally, breaking the odd tension that had shimmered between them just for a moment.

"Coffee? Oh, yes. That would be great," Gale said a little breathlessly. She made a serious effort to appear cool and poised as she leaned against the table's edge, but when she knocked over the pepper grinder with an airy wave of her hand, she cringed. "Oh, Lord. Look, just let me wash up and change out of these muddy sneakers, okay?"

She escaped, expecting at any moment to hear his derisive laughter following after her. What was happening to her? Normally she wasn't so disaster-prone, but lately, everything she went near seemed to fall apart.

In the bathroom, she splashed cold water over her face, and then stared at her dripping image. Surely those patches of red in her cheeks had been caused by the wind. It had turned decidedly colder while she'd been looking over the orchard and talking to the farmer about the possibility of taking pictures there. In her usual layers of cotton, silk and wool, her body had been warm enough, but her hands, feet and face had suffered.

Her hair. No wonder he'd been staring at her as if she'd sprouted an extra head! Plucking a twig and a patch of moss from the wild, dark mop, she reached for her brush and dragged it through the shoulder-length waves, grumbling at the effects of static electricity that sent it flying about her head.

"Now I know how Medusa got that way." Why couldn't she have been blessed with hair like Susan's? Smooth and straight, it invariably fell into place with a toss of the head, and never, *ever* tangled.

"In the study," Sax indicated when she rejoined him in the kitchen. He'd evidently taken both barbecue plates in and came back for the coffee pot. "I lit a fire in the fireplace, since you don't seem inclined to use the furnace."

He watched her reaction, the parade of expressions across her freshly scrubbed face. Why hadn't she simply told him that the oil bill was overdue? Because she'd been given money to pay it and had used it for her own purposes instead? And as if that weren't bad enough, she'd then tried to get at Olivia's account.

How could anyone who looked so guileless be so thoroughly unscrupulous?

"Mmm, this is nice," Gale murmured, curling up in the chair nearest the fireplace. In fact it was *very* nice. It was amazing how the presence of a particular person could alter the atmosphere of a whole house. She'd never felt quite as if she belonged at Saxon Hall—or anywhere else, for that matter. Now, in spite of all odds, she felt at ease, as if she'd just now come home. As scary as it was to admit it, she knew that it was Saxon who made all the difference.

"There was a stack of wood in the pump house, too far gone to put out much heat, unfortunately, but I cut enough new stuff to go with it." Sax removed the cover from his plate and examined the contents. Barbecued ribs was just one of the things he'd missed over the years. The Western version was good, but it bore little resemblance to this tender, succulent, hickory-smoked pork.

Neither of them spoke for several minutes. Firelight cast flattering shadows across the aged cherry paneling, and the smell of wood smoke mingled with the scent of barbecue sauce, coffee and the lotion Gale had smoothed on her hands and face.

Saxon filled both mugs, handed her one, and then leaned back in his chair, letting his long, work-hardened hands savor the warmth of the blue stoneware mug. "I suppose now that I'm home again, it might be a good idea if I took over some of the burden of running this place. It can't be much fun, having to look after a place this size. A girl your age should be out having a good time."

For the first time, he became aware of the tremendous amount of dignity inherent in her small frame, her rather grave features. It had been easy to overlook, all things considered.

"I'm hardly a girl, Saxon," Gale said quietly. "I'll be twenty-six in a few months, and as for having fun..."

"I'm sorry, Gale. Poor choice of words." The apology was sincere. Whatever else she might be, she'd been through some rough times these past few years, if what Billy had told him was true.

The business about Mal Chandler's financial problems and eventual death had been a real shock. He'd heard some brief mention of it on the news when it had happened, but no details. They'd been in the middle of a minor crisis on the ranch at the time, and he hadn't paid much attention.

As if the trauma of losing her parents the way she had weren't enough, she'd been in the middle of a lousy marriage that ended in yet another tragedy. Hell, she'd been little more than a kid.

He was beginning to understand why she might have gone off the rails, but understanding didn't mean condoning. Besides, he had to think of his father's interests. It seemed that no one else was looking after them.

"Gale—" Sax broke off, finding it hard to meet those clear, smoky-topaz eyes. What the devil did he say to her? I understand? You were under extreme stress?

Hell, so was he! These days, who wasn't? Larceny was no answer, and neither was forging checks. She'd really find out what stress was if she landed on her pretty little behind in a jail cell one of these days.

For the sake of—well, hell, for the sake of *something* or other, he'd have to do what he could to save her from herself.

Watching as she delicately demolished another hush puppy and licked her fingertips, he sighed heavily. There was nothing he could do tonight. Nothing he could do at all until he gained her confidence.

"Gale, did I tell you about the ranch I won in a poker game?"

During the following hour, Gale laughed more than she could remember having laughed in years. It wasn't that Sax deliberately set out to be funny—more as if he'd set out deliberately to take her mind off all her problems.

Of course, he had no way of knowing just how many problems she'd managed to accumulate. And she certainly wasn't about to dump them onto his broad shoulders, no matter how tempted she was. The man had come home after all these years to find his father desperately ill; she was sure he had enough problems of his own to deal with.

"Red socks?" she scoffed. "You mean he wouldn't fly a mission unless he was wearing his lucky socks?"

"Not necessarily wearing them. Sometimes he just stuffed one in his pocket. After awhile, someone in his crew got smart and taped one under his seat." Sax felt the warmth of the fireplace begin to seep into his bones. Once more he experienced that intriguing blend of tension and relaxation he'd noticed the first night he'd come here.

All glowing eyes and flushed cheeks, Gale was leaning forward, hanging onto his words with fascination. It was probably just an act, but he had to admit it was an effective one. Her rapt attention was extremely flattering, even if he knew it was deliberate.

Sax made up his mind to give her a little more rope. "You'd have to know Jay to understand. He'd been flying since he was a kid and figured he'd used up more than his share of luck a long time ago. That was the main reason he decided not to sign on for another hitch."

"But the ranch," Gale prompted. "If he was getting out of the service, what did he plan to do with the rest of his life?" She couldn't believe a man would gamble his livelihood on the turn of a card.

Although, come to think of it, was what her father had done much different? At least the ranch had been Jay's to gamble away.

Sax smiled, causing an odd little catch in Gale's breathing that was becoming all too familiar. "A few hundred acres of saltbush and shinnery oak wrapped up in rusty barbed wire," he said. "It'd been a losing proposition for years. The bank owned most of the machinery, and the cattle had long since been sold off to pay the taxes."

"But you won it?"

"Half interest, anyway. If you call it winning. At any rate, I took it, but only on the condition that Jay stay on and run the place. God knows, the last thing I knew anything about was running a ranch. I played polo a couple of seasons, but you can imagine how well that would have gone over out in the Oklahoma panhandle country."

"Oh, I don't know—polo can get pretty rough," Gale said, a smile teasing at the corners of her mouth as she pictured him on horseback.

"So can the guys on the Steppin' Creek Ranch," Sax said dryly. "Anyhow, since then, we've built the place up to where in a good year, we can almost break even."

Gale marveled that a man of Saxon's background could move from one arena to the next with such apparent ease. She'd discovered that he'd graduated from Duke University, served in the coast guard like his father, and for the past several years, had been a rancher. If he was bothered by the hardscrabble operation he'd described, there was nothing to indicate the fact.

"Maybe you should turn it into a dude ranch," she suggested.

"Are you serious?" Sax thought of the nickname he'd earned the first time he'd showed up in full Western regalia. "Dudes like their creature comforts. We're just now getting used to having indoor plumbing."

Laughing, Gale propped her arms on her knees and leaned forward, eyes sparkling. She couldn't remember the last time she'd enjoyed herself so much. The emptiness that had always seemed to hover just out of reach, threatening to envelope her if she ever let down her guard, was nowhere in evidence tonight.

From out in the foyer came the wheezing sound of the tall clock as it sonorously began to sound the hour. "Ten," Sax said when it had finally finished. "I expect I'd better let you go."

"Oh, please—not yet." The protest escaped before she could help herself.

I'd better let you go. How many times had she called from school, eager to hear her mother's voice, willing to listen to endless details of committee work, or garden club gossip—anything, as long as she could feel close to home for just a little while. "I guess I'd better let you go," her mother would say as soon as the amenities had been exchanged.

How's father?

Busy, as usual.

How's Susan?

I'm sure she's just fine, dear, and now I'd better let you go.

Casting one last look at the glowing logs, Gale said a little wistfully, "Maybe if you bank the fire, it'll last until morning."

"I'll cut more firewood tomorrow," Sax promised. "Good night, Gale."

"Good night, Sax," She sighed unconsciously as she collected their dinner things and reluctantly left the room.

Gale rose early, dressed quickly and went in search of breakfast. At least, she told herself that was the reason she'd hurried, but it couldn't explain her look of bright expectancy as she pushed open the swinging door. Nor her look of disappointment when she found the kitchen empty and half a pot of coffee waiting on the warmer, indicating that she hadn't been the first one up.

Fine. That was just fine. She needed to plan her day anyway, and she did her best thinking over breakfast. The last thing she needed was to have someone chattering about dude ranches and superstitious helicopter pilots while she was trying to concentrate.

The orchard was going to be perfect for the scene in which Tripod, the three-legged elephant who'd escaped from a cruel trainer, met Boy and Golly. She'd planned to have him discover Boy trapped in a tree and lift him down with his trunk. The scale would be a bit tricky, because the mutilated plush elephant she'd discovered in a trash can and written into the story wasn't quite as large as she would have liked.

Still, with a little ingenuity, she could make it work. The orderly rows of apple trees in the background would lend perspective—it should do the trick.

And trickery was her forte. *Trompe l'oeil.* "The art of deception," she murmured as she planned the best way to merge fantasy with real life.

But then, wasn't fantasy real, too? If seeing was believing, and Gale could show people things in such a way that fantasy appeared real, then... Well, as far as she knew, no one had come up with a definitive answer yet, so she may as well invent her own reality.

Saxon loaded the Jeep with firewood and drove back to the house. He'd spent the day clearing away dead limbs and dismantling the old kennels, part of which had already collapsed. He didn't know why he bothered, except that physical labor was a hard habit to break.

It was as good a reason as any. In fact it was a damned sight more acceptable than the one that kept pushing to the forefront of his mind every time he pictured a small woman huddled in a large chair, firelight shimmering like rainbows in her hair, and turning her eyes into pure magic.

The woman was a witch. Even knowing who she was, what she'd been through and what she was up to, he found it almost impossible to keep his thoughts under control.

According to Billy, everyone in town had known that marriage hadn't trimmed Jeff's sails at all. If that's what Richard had been hoping for, he must have been sorely disappointed.

Jeff had been a fool! Nearly ten years had separated them, but Sax had known him in the way he'd known everyone else in the area, by sight, if not personally.

Jeff had run with a younger set, a wild bunch that had earned a pretty bad reputation even before they were out of high school. Sax seemed to recall that he'd been sent off to a military school once, but it hadn't stuck. He'd always been in and out of trouble. Richard had gone to bat for him more than once, and Sax had assumed at the time that it was because he'd been his secretary's son.

Now Sax backed the Jeep up to the small porch that let into the utility room and started unloading firewood, his mind still on a situation that was growing increasingly perplexing. He didn't want his judgment of Gale to be influenced by the memories of Jeff's wildness.

Nor did he care to be influenced by whatever it was about her that made him wish they'd met a thousand miles away, with no previous ties.

Oh, hell, that was his body talking, not his brain! Maybe he'd better split another few cords of hickory.

Her car was gone, he noted. He'd deliberately refrained from asking what she did with herself all day. It was his survival instinct, probably, warning him not to get too involved. It wouldn't be the first time a man had lost his head over a pair of smoky-brown eyes and a husky laugh that tickled his spine like warm fingertips.

The wood stacked, he washed up in the kitchen and put through a call to the ranch. Tully answered, telling him Jay was mending a busted chute over in the west pasture.

"Your lady friend's been callin' out here regular, wantin' to know when you was coming back," the old cook said slyly.

"What'd you tell her?" Sax chuckled. He was used to being ribbed about his occasional weekends in Guymon. Enid Brachman, an attractive redhead about his own age, worked as a receptionist for a firm of lawyers there.

"Told her you wuz married now, and expectin' six-tuplets, and if she was looking for a good man, I'd be more'n willin' to oblige."

"Did you tell her you were bald as an egg, mean as a cottonmouth, and the last time you took a bath, we had to hog-tie you and throw you in the creek?"

"There's no call to go gettin' personal."

Sax laughed, passed on a message for his partner and hung up, feeling suspended between the two halves of his life. Roots could be frustrating things when they'd been yanked up from one location and transplanted to another.

It was almost dark when Gale drove up to the garage and switched off the engine. She'd gone by Laurel Hill on her way home, and then stopped off at the grocer's. Saxon had given her money to pay for food that first night; not knowing how long it was meant to last, she'd used it as sparingly as she could without his getting suspicious.

There was no one in the house. Mrs. McCrary had come and gone, leaving her apron draped over the broom handle and a broken teacup in the trash as evidence of having been there. Gale sighed. Olivia was going to have to do something about that woman.

Meanwhile, she'd better check to see if Sax's linens had been changed. The housekeeper could easily have forgotten about the upstairs bedroom that was now in use.

Just as Gale had suspected, nothing had been done. The bed had been neatly spread, the corners militarily correct, and three inches of flowered sheet hung out on one side from under the quilted cover.

She peeled back the bedclothes, stripped off the sheets and pillow slips and balled them up. Then, leaving the bed to air for a few minutes, she went into the bathroom and gathered up the used towels. She worked methodically, forcing herself to ignore the small reminders of the man who slept in the bed, bathed in the tub and brushed his thick, pewter-colored hair before the dresser mirror.

There was a tantalizing hint of a crisp, masculine scent hovering in the room, and she breathed deeply, her hand growing still as she used a pillow slip to dust the dresser and the bedside table.

Odd, how stimulating a fragrance could be. She'd sniffed at the samples in Jeff's men's fashion magazines, read the romantic little vignettes advertising a particular men's cologne—and sighed, trying to summon a few erotic fantasies. The fledgling dreams she'd brought with her into marriage had quickly withered and died.

But now, after breathing in one whiff of the crisp, clean scent Saxon used, a woodsy, spicy fragrance that she'd never have described as seductive, she was imagining all sorts of things!

The linen closet was at the end of the hall, near the stairway, which was inconvenient, since she slept on the first floor. But it was hardly worth the effort to relocate. Gale collected a matched set of brown percale monogrammed sheets and a fresh set of towels, also monogrammed, and carried them back to the bedroom. As soon as she finished doing Saxon's rooms, she'd start the spaghetti sauce and then hop into the shower. Her knees, elbows and feet were cold, chapped and probably muddy. Being an outdoor photographer wasn't the cleanest job in the world, especially this time of year.

She'd just snapped a sheet over the bed when Sax appeared in the doorway. The sheet settled crookedly and slithered to the floor as she looked up, startled. "I didn't hear you come in," she said, trying not to look as flustered as she actually was.

Sax stared at the wild-haired waif in the mud-stained corduroys who was leaning over his bed, her cheeks glowing like candy apples. His body, ignoring the windblown hair and the asexual clothes, reacted to the pale band of skin where her sweater had ridden up in the back.

This was crazy! The woman dressed with all the allure of a twelve-year-old street urchin, and already his palms were growing sweaty.

He cleared his throat and shifted his weight to the other foot. "Sorry," he said tightly. "I didn't mean to startle you. My boots were muddy, so I left 'em in the utility room."

"I can do this later. Why don't I just wait until— You probably want to— I put out some clean towels in the bathroom," she finally got out.

"You don't have to do this at all. The housekeeper can do it, or I will."

"Mrs. McCrary forgot," Gale said, relieved to find that her tongue was working again. At least she'd managed to complete a three-word sentence without stuttering.

"Then I'll wait until she comes back."

"But I've already stripped the bed. I may as well put on clean sheets."

"Then I'll help you," Sax said resignedly. "Next time you consider my linens need changing, just let me know. I'll do it myself." He moved to the other side of the bed and gathered up the sheet that had slid onto the floor. With a deft flick of his strong wrists, he placed it squarely over the mattress.

"Well done," Gale congratulated.

"Comes from spending hundreds of hours practicing with a lariat," Sax said modestly. "Oklahoma's Will Rogers's territory." A look of amusement gradually replaced the tension that had sharpened the planes of his face.

Gale bent over and swept the excess yardage under the mattress. "Comes from years of bed making under the eagle eye of housemothers and camp councillors," she quipped.

They made short work of spreading the rest of the bed, and as Saxon reached for the quilted coverlet, he said, "About dinner tonight—if you haven't started anything, we could go out somewhere."

Gale automatically extended her hand to catch the heavy spread. She fumbled and tried again, and when her fingers tangled with Saxon's, she snatched them back, rubbing them as if she'd been stung.

He grinned from across the broad expanse of the king-size bed. "Sorry. I'll spread; you tuck, okay?"

In no time at all the chore was finished. "I thought you might enjoy a break," Sax said. "I never intended to put you to so much trouble when I moved in here."

"It's no trouble," Gale protested a little too quickly. "After all, you split all that wood and you do pay for the groceries."

"That was our agreement, but that doesn't mean we can't take a night off now and then."

Gale considered his offer. If she were honest with herself, she'd have to admit that she'd been looking forward to another cozy dinner in front of the fireplace, looking forward to it a little too much, in fact.

All the more reason to go out tonight, she told herself firmly. "The Copper Kettle's open until nine tonight."

Sax found himself fascinated by the parade of expressions that had flickered across her features. If he hadn't known better, he'd have thought she had one of the most open faces he'd ever seen on a woman. "I was thinking more in terms of someplace like the club," he said.

Gale nibbled her lower lip. "The Copper Kettle has good food, and their prices are—"

"Gale, I'm not exactly a pauper," Sax said, amused in spite of himself. "I think I can swing a dinner for two at Hunting Ridge Club." Watching her reaction closely, he added, "The ranch isn't my sole means of support, you know. My mother set up a trust for me when I was born. Luckily, it's done pretty well over the years, thanks to some sound investments."

The minute the words left his lips, Sax cursed himself for being such a conniver. He'd been deliberately trying to set her up. Maybe she deserved it, but it wasn't up to him to judge her.

More and more he was coming to think that he didn't want to know how much she'd stolen from his father's house. He didn't *want* to know how far she'd go in her search for security.

Standing under the needle spray of his shower a few minutes later, he tried with only limited success to convince himself that that was all the more reason to go on testing her.

Chapter Five

Gale switched on her blow dryer and aimed it at her towel-dried hair. It would make it totally unmanageable, but perhaps she could do something with braids and pins and a few well-placed combs. The moisturizer on her face did little to ease the sting of too many hours spent outside in the raw wind and brilliant mountain sunshine. For her next book, she might consider an indoor setting.

As fantasies went, *The Bridge to Golly's House* was remarkably realistic; if it rained on her, then it rained on Golly and Boy. If the sun beat down on her head, then their heads were equally vulnerable.

But rain or shine, Gale had never felt as vulnerable as she did tonight.

It had been ages since she'd dressed in anything more formal than a pair of flannel slacks, a cashmere sweater and loafers. The pale gray knit with the flowing skirt and the cowl neck was a perfect foil for the wide lizard belt with its jeweled buckle. The matching shoes had skyscraper heels—she only hoped she didn't trip and break something. The last time she'd worn the outfit had been at a dinner Richard and Olivia had given for her and Jeff soon after they'd been married.

Was she overdoing it? Probably so, but if she had to suffer the wagging tongues at the club, it would help to know that she was looking her best. It had been ages since she'd been there, and most of the members had been friends of her parents.

Leaning over from the waist, Gale gathered a handful of flyaway hair and began braiding. When she was done, she anchored the coil on top of her head with several pins and the sterling combs Susan had given her for her birthday.

It wasn't as if this was a real date, she reminded herself firmly. It was only the cook's night out, and in any case, she was a bit beyond the dewy-eyed romance stage.

Better for her if she'd never entered it!

Sax was waiting for her in the study. He'd laid the fireplace and carefully replaced the screen. Now, turning to greet her, he brushed off his hands, his gaze moving over her with growing appreciation.

Gale's eyes were doing some appreciating of their own. Standing just inside the door, she clutched her coat, a cranberry-colored Chesterfield, and wondered what it was about one particular man out of two thousand others that could turn a woman's knees to jelly. She'd always had a creative imagination, but it had never before gone in for *this* sort of fantasy.

Sax wore an ivory shirt with a sober tie and a gray suit that skimmed the breadth of his shoulders, merely hinting at the lean, hard body beneath.

A hint was more than enough, Gale thought sinkingly. She shifted the coat she held from one damp hand to the other. What was happening to her? She hadn't reacted this way to a man since the night Jeff had singled her out for attention at the club dance right after she'd come back from Susan's wedding.

Surely she wasn't going to make that mistake again!

"I think this is where one of us is supposed to say 'pass and be recognized,'" Sax remarked with a look of amusement. He had a way of almost smiling, Gale decided, that made the Mona Lisa look positively surly.

"It's been so long since I wore a dress, I'd almost forgotten how to put on a pair of panty hose," she confessed, and then felt her cheeks start to burn again.

"Blushing? At a little word like panty hose?" Sax teased, removing the coat from her hands and holding it so that she could slide her arms into the sleeves.

Gale balled her fists and rammed them through. "I haven't blushed since I was twelve years old. It's not my fault my skin reacts this way to too much sun and wind!"

He laughed aloud, and Gale felt the sound reverberate deep inside her, like the rumbling bass notes of a massive pipe organ.

They took Richard's car, and Gale was glad she didn't have to suffer the draftiness of the rag-topped Jeep. According to Sax, the Saab needed an occasional outing to keep it from deteriorating. "I'm afraid Dad won't be needing it again anytime soon."

He sent her a quick look. "Maybe you'd better see about selling it."

Gale eased her feet out of the snug gray lizard pumps and curled her toes into the thick carpeting. There'd been a time when Richard's handyman had kept both the grounds and all the family's vehicles in perfect condition. He'd been let go soon after Richard had gone into the hospital. "Olivia was going to, but then this trip came up so suddenly. She's been a little distracted lately, trying to do a hundred things at once and then moping around in her room without seeing anyone for days. It's understandable, I suppose, when you consider all she's been through."

Sax refrained from reminding Gale that she hadn't exactly gotten off lightly these past two years, herself. As for Olivia, he'd found lately that his resentment against the woman who had replaced his mother in Richard's affections had faded until it was hardly worth hanging on to. Olivia must have been even younger than Gale when their affair had begun—separated from her husband, and with a child on the way. After all the years of playing the double role of secretary and mistress, she could hardly be blamed for jumping at the chance to be Richard Evanshaw's wife.

Nor was there any reason to believe she'd been anything but a good wife for the past eleven years. Altogether, he admitted reluctantly, that added up to a lot of loyalty. For that much, at least, he owed her.

Breaking the silence that had accompanied them for the last several miles, he said, "According to Billy Trent, the Hunting Ridge Club still serves the best filet of beef around."

Gale would rather have had chicken-fried steak at the Copper Kettle. She felt comfortable there. The staff and the regulars had seen her around enough to take her presence for granted. Like most members of their social set, the Chandlers had belonged to the club. Neither Gale nor Susan had gone there often, as it was geared more to her parents' generation than theirs.

Remembering one such visit, she confided, "I saw you there once, you know."

"At the club? When was that?"

"I must have been about thirteen. I know I was home for vacation for a change because the aunt I usually stayed with in Connecticut was trying to have a discreet affair. I was definitely odd man out at her house that spring. Anyway, Daddy insisted on taking Susan for lunch that day, and I begged to go along, and there you were."

Sax felt amusement—and something more—to think that she'd remembered him after all these years. "How'd you know who I was?"

"Someone must have mentioned your name." It had been Richard, actually. He'd stopped by the table while they were having dessert and mentioned to Susan that he had a son about her age who'd enjoy meeting her. Even before Richard had pointed him out across the room, Gale had known which one he was. Saxon Evanshaw had stood out in a room full of people even then, both for his looks and for the way he carried himself.

When she'd first met him, Richard had still had a vestige of that same type of energy. In Sax it had been developed to the point where one could actually feel it when he entered a room.

"Come to think of it," he mused, "I might have seen you, too." He'd definitely seen Susan. So had every other male in the room. He'd been only marginally aware of two other people at the same table. "Pigtails? Braces? Glasses?"

Gale made a wry face. "How sweet of you to remember in such intimate detail."

Sax laughed, and she felt a fluttery weakness invade her limbs. "If it's any comfort to you," he said, "the braces did a wonderful job. As for your hair..." Glancing at her, he pretended to ponder the problem. "I think I prefer what you've done to it tonight."

"And my designer glasses? You know—lenses by the local bottling company?"

It occurred to her that she must wear contacts, which probably accounted for the hypnotic quality of her eyes. One more illusion gone. "I can't say I blame you for switching to contacts."

"Contacts? I'm not wearing anything—well, not on my eyes, at least," she amended. "I'd broken my nose trying to rappel down the administration building, and for some reason, it caused my eyes to cross. I had to wear glasses and do a lot of tiresome eye exercises to straighten them out again. Daddy refused to look at me, but Susan used to bring me all sorts of treats to bribe me to do them. There was this dessert the club used to make—blueberry clafouti. I wonder if they still make it."

Skillfully guiding the heavy car along the twisted mountain road, Sax chuckled softly. "If they do, we'll both indulge. Oh, and Gale—if it's any consolation, all those exercises were worth the effort." He almost wished she had been wearing contacts. Smoky-topaz ones that could be held accountable for luring a man to the very edge of destruction. Even knowing she wasn't what she appeared to be, he had trouble keeping his wits around her.

A few minutes later they pulled into the driveway of the rambling rock and cedar structure that nestled in the midst of some two hundred acres of private forest land and well-kept greens. Sax had checked to be sure Richard's membership was still active. Otherwise, he'd planned on using Billy's. Now he pulled under the carport, waited for the attendant to help Gale out of the car and then handed over the keys.

When he noticed the wave of curious glances that followed their progress to the main lobby, off which the dining rooms were located, it occurred to him for the first time that this might not have been a particularly wise move. It had been habit, more than anything else, that had made him call the club for reservations, but even before he gave his name at the reservations desk, it was obvious that people had noticed their entrance. Whispers swept through the room like an autumn wind through dry leaves. Two names rose above the susurrus again and again—Malcolm Chandler and Jeff Evanshaw. Saxon felt Gale stiffen beside him.

His jaw tightened as he waited for the maître d' to run practiced eyes down his list. If he'd thought it wouldn't cause even more talk, he'd have taken her away from there right then. He didn't give a damn about himself—his hide was too tough to matter, but he wouldn't have subjected her to this if he'd realized it would happen.

Holding her small hand tucked protectively under his arm, he could feel her fingers digging into his flesh. Turning his back on a small group standing around the baby grand, he leaned over and whispered in her ear.

"Isn't that old Harvey Motsinger in the red vest? I ran out of gas with his daughter one night when I was about seventeen, and he threatened me with several interesting, little-known laws if I ever so much as spoke to her again."

Gale managed a laugh, and then wished she hadn't as she tried to ignore the whispers that followed their progress through the main dining room. She'd hoped that any gossip surrounding Jeff's infidelities and her parents' deaths would've died down by now.

There'd been nothing she could do about it then; there was nothing she could do about it now—other than hibernate for the rest of her life, and she refused to do that. Tonight she'd simply have to pretend again—pretend that she was neither Mal Chandler's daughter nor Jeff Evanshaw's widow. Instead she'd be just a woman spending a few pleasant hours with the man of her choice.

They were led to one of the more secluded nooks, this one done in melon pink, with hunting prints and a modest trophy display. "It hasn't changed a bit since the last time I was in here," Sax remarked after their waiter had left with their bar order.

"I don't think I've ever seen this room before. We didn't come here a lot."

"Where does the younger set hang out nowadays?" As he watched the play of expressions on the face of the woman seated across from him, Sax was conscious, not for the first time, of a pervasive look of sadness about her. Understandable, he supposed. Still, it had been a year; she should be coming out of it by now. So why did there always seem to be a shadow lying just under the surface of her eyes?

In answer to his question, Gale named a night spot out on the main highway that had been notorious for as long as Sax could remember. "Jeff usually met his friends at the Dirty Angel. Sometimes they'd drive out to Stoney's, or The Fast Track or to a private party somewhere."

"What about you, didn't you go?" He found it impossible to picture her in any of the dives she'd mentioned.

"Not often. I've never been very good in social situations. According to Jeff, I can bring down a perfectly good party just by walking into the room." She smiled ruefully, glad of the distraction when the waiter appeared with their drinks.

"Soda with a twist for the lady and bourbon for the gentleman. Would you like to order dinner now, or shall I come back later?"

They ordered, with Gale finally deferring to Sax's judgment. Once the waiter had gone, she lifted her chin and announced with soft defiance, "Just because I let you choose for me doesn't mean that I'm always this docile. The trouble is, it all looked so wonderful I couldn't make up my mind. It was either you or eenie, meenie, miny, mo."

"I'll bear it in mind," Saxon said with mock gravity. Actually, he'd been rather touched by her look of pleasurable excitement as she'd pored over the menu. The club's choices weren't that extensive, nor all that unusual.

They carefully kept to impersonal topics for the remainder of the evening, and Sax found himself growing more and more curious about her relationship with Jeff. For the life of him, he couldn't see why a woman like Gale Chandler would have been attracted to the flashy, willful boy he remembered Jeff Donner as having been.

There was the money, of course. With Sax out of the way, Jeff had stood to inherit everything Richard owned, which, even after Richard's retirement and the merger of Evanshaw Furniture with another firm, was a considerable fortune. In order to keep up with all Richard's various investments, Tad Benton had left the firm when Richard had stepped down. That had been the same year Saxon had left home.

But then, as Mal Chandler's daughter, Gale would have been wealthy in her own right. Sax had no idea what her actual financial circumstances had been at the time of her marriage, but certainly her expectations had been healthy enough.

Unless she'd suspected what her father was up to and decided to play it safe. According to Billy, the Chandler scandal had broken less than a year after Gale had married Jeff. Susan seemed to have bailed out before the ship went down; was there any reason to think Gale had been less shrewd?

When their waiter returned after their plates were cleared Gale asked about her favorite dessert.

"It's one of our specialties, ma'am. And I can also personally recommend the coconut blancmange and the pecan pie." The tall youth in the short red coat looked from one to the other, and deferred once more to Saxon. "Sir?"

"Bring us one of each."

"Saxon!" Gale leaned forward, a look of slightly horrified delight on her face.

"I'll help you if you can't handle it alone."

"Who's going to take care of me when I wake up in the middle of the night with a stomachache?"

His lips twitched. "I'll take full responsibility, I promise."

As it turned out, Gale had little more than a taste of each delectable dessert. It was Saxon who finished them off, one after the other. "Coconut, pecans and blueberries. If you'd ever sampled Tully's baking, you'd understand," he said by way of explanation on the way home. "His idea of cake baking is to dump a few handfuls of sugar into his basic biscuit recipe. You have to dunk the results in coffee to keep from breaking a tooth."

"I'm not great at desserts either, unless you happen to like liquid cheesecake."

Sax chuckled as he avoided a pothole in the driveway. Moonlight gleamed on the mustard-yellow sedan parked just outside the garage door. "I could leave the Jeep outside and make room for your car. I don't know why you didn't do that yourself, anyway." He pulled in beside the muddy vehicle Richard had used at one time to check the boundaries of his property, and switched off the engine.

"Thanks, but she'd die of shock." Actually, she'd considered parking it inside at one time, if only to fill the empty space that had once been claimed by Jeff's Ferrari so that Richard and Olivia wouldn't have to avert their eyes each time they entered the garage.

Evidently, Shupp, the handyman, had had the same idea. He'd started parking the Jeep inside, and after that, it had hardly seemed important. "She's a lot tougher than she looks."

"Wait until the temperature gets down below zero and she doesn't want to wake up in the morning. Maybe you'll change your tune then." Sax sighed when he realized that she had him personifying a piece of mustard-yellow machinery.

Gale buried her chin in her scarf and smiled as she waited for Sax to unlock the door. By the time the most severe winter weather set in, neither one of them would be here to worry about whether or not her car would start. She'd have found a place of her own, and Saxon would be back on his ranch complaining about Tully's desserts.

"Would you like to have coffee in the study?" Sax asked. It was barely eleven o'clock. Gale thought longingly of the fire he'd laid before they'd left for the club.

"I'd better not," she said reluctantly. "I want to get an early start tomorrow, and coffee at this hour might not be a good idea."

"An early start?" Actually, he was just as glad she'd turned down the offer. He was beginning to understand why fraternizing with the enemy was considered risky business.

"Oh—just a few things I wanted to do. Nothing important," she said lightly.

"Maybe we could team up," Sax suggested, his eyes narrowing slightly as he noted her evasiveness. "I've got a few errands, too. We could combine forces and then go by Laurel Hill to see Dad."

Gale felt one of the silver combs holding up the heavy weight of her hair begin to slide. Absently, she tugged it out and then plucked out the others, allowing the released braid to fall over one shoulder. "Maybe I'd better just stick to my own schedule," she said a little regretfully. She wasn't about to expose her efforts to Sax's critical comments.

"Whatever you say," he replied. "Then I'll see you for dinner tomorrow night, if not before."

Suddenly, the comfortable ease that had sprung up between them during dinner seemed to dissipate like a wisp of wood smoke. Gale hated to relinquish it—that tentative feeling of friendship that had emerged so unexpectedly at the club as they'd laughed about the dreadful watercolor of Roan Mountain that had been painted by the wife of a board member and donated in loving memory of her mother. They'd even been in agreement that the music drifting in from the piano bar was surprisingly good.

She'd probably just imagined it, she told herself a few minutes later in her bedroom as she stepped out of the toe-cramping shoes. Imagined the whole thing—those long, thoughtful glances across the candlelit table, the time when his hand had collided with hers on the salt shaker and they'd both nearly jumped out of their skins. A creative mind was all very well, but there was no point in letting her imagination run hog-wild.

Quickly she slipped out of her dress and hung it up. Shivering in the chilly air of her bedroom, she finished undressing and pulled on a yellow flannel nightgown. Getting on cozy terms with Saxon Evanshaw would have been a mistake in any case, she rationalized as she brushed her teeth, toes curled against the cold tile floor.

As she parted the covers to slide into bed, she couldn't help but wonder if Sax was still in the study, nursing a drink, watching the firelight cast flickering shadows across the room.

She'd done the smart thing. If she'd hung around much longer, she'd have been pouring out all her worries onto his accommodating shoulders. After which, it would have been only a matter of time before she'd have started telling him all about how she'd been selling off his family heirlooms.

Great. That would make a wonderful impression, wouldn't it? She'd be lucky if he didn't have her up on criminal charges before she even got a chance to explain. She knew she'd been justified. Well—*sort* of justified. But would Saxon?

Gale had always considered herself an excellent manager when it came to money. Not that she'd ever had any great sums. There'd been her school allowance, plus the usual checks for birthdays and Christmases.

"Buy yourself something you really want, dear," her mother had always said, and Gale had usually put most of her birthday checks into camera equipment and supplies.

After she and Jeff had been married, their only income had been an allowance from Richard, a situation which Gale had found extremely uncomfortable. She'd quickly discovered that Jeff had no intention of working as long as anyone would subsidize him, but when she'd brought up the prospect of looking for work herself, she'd run head on into a stone wall. It seemed the Evanshaw women never worked for money.

Gale had barely restrained herself from reminding both Jeff and Richard that Olivia had worked as a secretary. It was common knowledge, even though it was seldom mentioned. But then, Olivia hadn't been *Mrs. Evanshaw* at the time.

She'd backed down, of course. No one stood up to Richard. His own son was proof of what happened when anyone tried.

* * *

Gale woke to the sound of the grandfather clock. Clinging to sleep, she counted four bongs, but it could have been going on forever. What had awakened her? Hardly the clock; it was one of those household noises that faded into the background from repetition.

Darn! She was wide awake. What was worse, she knew she'd never get back to sleep until she'd gone over the house and checked to see that everything was all right. What if someone had broken in? It was no secret that she was out here all alone, easy pickings for anyone who cared to try their hand at breaking and entering.

She slid out of bed, raking the floor with one foot in search of her slippers. Elusive as ever, they were probably hiding under the bed. With the possibility of a burglar in the house, Gale was half-tempted to join them there.

Without turning on a light, she felt for her robe and threw it around her shoulders, slipping silently out the door while she struggled to ease her flannel-clad arms into the wool sleeves.

The dread of something like this happening had been hovering in the back of her consciousness ever since Olivia had left her in charge, but with so many other problems cropping up each day, she'd forgotten to worry about it. Now she didn't even have a glimmer of an idea what to do.

There wasn't a gun in the house, and even if there had been, she'd have been too frightened to try to use it. A flashlight was the best she could come up with at short notice. If someone really was sneaking around inside, she might be able to blind him just long enough to lock him in and call for help.

Not until she was halfway across the foyer did it occur to her that, intruder notwithstanding, she was no longer alone in the house. Saxon was sleeping upstairs. Why the devil should she be risking her neck when the responsibility was rightfully his?

Too late now. Saxon was upstairs and she was downstairs, and from the sound of it, so was their intruder. In the study, to be more precise. She could see a sliver of light under the door, and she paused to shift her grip on the flashlight.

A light? So much for her plan to blind him.

With her hand on the knob, she wavered for a moment. Was it really worth risking her neck? She could still creep upstairs and wake Saxon. He was big enough to hide behind, and she liked the sound of the odds a lot better.

But she didn't like the sounds that were coming from inside the study. Someone was going through Richard's desk. One drawer always jammed—the upper right, the one where the stationery supplies were kept—and the only way to open it was to hit it with the butt of your hand and jerk it open. That was probably what had wakened her.

Goodness knows what was in the other drawers. Important papers? The combination to a safe? There was only one thing to do, under the circumstances, and Gale did it.

A moment later she clung to the open door as the excess adrenaline seeped from her system. "Do you have any idea how close you came to being blinded by a flashlight and then bopped on the head?" she demanded furiously.

Saxon stared at the white-faced creature clutching the chrome-plated flashlight. Her eyes were blazing, her stance militant, in spite of the fact that the collar of that yellow tent she was wearing was rucked up on one side, and several inches of it were hanging unevenly below her bathrobe.

Two small bare feet protruded, toes curling on the cool floor, and Sax's lips twitched. "I didn't mean to wake you up," he said gently. "I was looking for stationery and a stamp."

"Yes, well . . ." Gale came into the room, moving instinctively to the paler area where the rug was supposed to be. It was like backing up to a cold fireplace.

"What happened to your slippers?" Sax asked. He, too, had noticed the way she'd sought the comfort of the rug that was no longer there.

Dammit! Maybe it hadn't been the letter he needed to write to Enid that had brought him down here. More likely it was a subconscious attempt to remind himself of just how much this little hustler was capable of. When he was with her, she had an unfortunate way of making him forget why he was here in the first place.

"My slippers?" Gale placed one foot on top of the other, wondering what *he* was scowling about. *She* was the one who'd been scared out of her wits. "It hardly mattered where they were when I thought someone was down here looking for goodness knows what!"

"So you were going to blind me and bop me, right?"

As Gale watched, a muscle that had tensed along his jaw relaxed. Warily, she lowered herself to the arm of the couch and pulled her feet up under the warm cover of her gown. "I don't know about the bopping. My real plan was to flash the light in your eyes, slam the door and lock you in while I called the sheriff. But then, you already had the light on, so it wouldn't have worked anyway, would it?''

"And you came barging in here anyway? Fearless little soul, aren't you?'' Sax slid the drawer shut. The letter to Enid could wait another day—at any rate, he wasn't certain what he wanted to say to her.

"Chicken to the core. I've never had a burglar before. Next time, I'll have my act together.''

He'd changed into his jeans, she noted, and a black flannel shirt that he hadn't bothered to button. Nor was he wearing an undershirt. The body hair visible down the open front was sable dark, with no gray as far as she could tell.

Gale cradled her burning cheeks in the palms of her cold hands, tinglingly aware that Sax was watching her watching him. This was what happened when a person woke unexpectedly in the middle of the night. She lost all touch with reality. "Aren't you . . . cold?'' she asked in a voice that didn't even sound like her own.

"Cold? No, I'm not cold. Are you?''

He watched her. She watched him. One of his hands was rhythmically stroking the rounded corner of the desk, and Gale couldn't seem to tear her eyes away from the long, square-tipped fingers, or the light scattering of dark hair on the back. His wrists looked extremely powerful, yet they were shapely, as were his muscular forearms. He had neither buttoned the cuffs of his long-sleeved shirt, nor turned them back. They hung loose, now revealing, now concealing, as his palm slid over the satiny surface of the walnut desk.

Suddenly, she was overwhelmingly tired. Her shoulders drooped, her head tipped back and she closed her eyes. This whole bizarre affair had to be some obscure form of midnight madness. Gale told herself that she was one of those pragmatic early-to-bed, early-to-rise women who went a little haywire when her biological clock got out of kilter.

"I don't know about you, but I'm going back to bed," she said with a barely concealed yawn. When Sax didn't reply, she opened her eyes to discover that he'd moved silently around the desk to stand in front of her. "As soon as you get out of my way," she added pointedly.

Saxon's hand moved up to hover a hair's breadth from her face, so close she could feel the radiant heat. Without touching her face, they moved down to her shoulders, and there they settled. Then, with no effort at all, he toppled her against his chest.

Gale released the breath she wasn't even aware of having held. It came out in a long, shuddering sigh, and once more she allowed her eyes to drift shut, as if by closing them she could deny what was happening to her.

She could feel the late-night stubble as he brushed his face against her hair. Then he began to stroke her back, sliding flannel against skin in a sensuous caress that melted her resistance like butter on a hot stove. Raising her arms, she settled them around his hips as she rested her head against his chest.

"Witch," she thought he whispered. "Bewitching little..."

The last word was lost to her ears as he lifted her and brought his mouth down on hers at the same time. She didn't care. She wasn't interested in words. For now, she only wanted to be held. Held against a warm, hard body, by sheltering, comforting arms, kissed by a man who fanned to life coals that had long since burned down to gray ash.

"Too tempting—" he murmured against her parted lips. Then, without lifting his mouth from hers, he moved around the arm of the couch, settling himself into its cushioned comfort with her on his lap.

"Put your arms around my neck," he commanded softly, and when she complied, he ran his hands down her sides, exploring the narrow cage of her ribs, her tiny waist and the gentle flare of her hips. Gale told herself it was only her feverish imagination that made her think his fingertips had brushed against the sides of her breasts. She wanted his hands there.

Dear Lord, such exquisite torture! How was it possible to feel this way about a man she hardly knew? She'd never felt this way before, never dreamed she could! Jeff had been her first lover, and while the anticipation had been heady enough for any woman, the realization—for her, at least—had fallen depressingly short of her expectations.

Evidently, Jeff had agreed with her. After the first few months, he'd seldom bothered her when he came home late at night.

Without even realizing what she was doing, she slipped a hand inside Sax's shirt to curl her fingers against the resilient muscles of his chest. As she felt the heavy beat of his heart under her hand, what had begun as sheer sexual tension took on a deeper aspect, one she couldn't begin to fathom. Again she felt that odd sense of recognition, as if what was happening to her had been inevitable from the very beginning.

Sax stroked the sensitive hollow at the back of her neck, sending a fresh flurry of tremors down her spine. She was dimly aware of the release of the single button at the back of her gown, and then he tugged it loose, trying to slip his hand inside the neck. "Do you always wear straitjackets like this to bed?'' he muttered, sounding half-amused, half-exasperated.

"Only if I want to keep from freezing.'' She twisted her neck to keep from being strangled as he worked one hand in as far as her shoulder.

Sax eased his hand out again, and sighed heavily. "This isn't going to work, is it? Unless you'd care to join me somewhere where we can, as the saying goes, slip into something comfortable.''

Reluctantly, Gale sat up. She was still seated on his lap, still acutely aware of the aroused male body beneath her. "I can't imagine how this happened, Saxon. I mean, why we—''

"Can't you?'' Sax interrupted softly.

With unsteady fingers, she pushed back her hair. Sliding carefully off his lap, she began straightening her clothes while he looked on, the sardonic gleam in his eyes doing nothing at all to help the situation. He wasn't making it any easier for her. "No, I can't,'' she snapped. "I came in here because I thought someone was trying to burgle the place, and that's the only reason!''

"If you say so.'' He shrugged. "Can't blame me for getting the wrong idea, though, Gale. When a man and a woman living together alone out in the country share a candlelit dinner for two, and then meet again at midnight—when she's all soft and flushed from bed, and her lips have that certain look about them, then a man would have to be a fool not to pick up his cue.''

"I was *not* soft and flushed!'' she argued, clutching her robe tightly around her. "And what's more, my lips didn't have any look at all about them.''

"And I'm no fool, Gale.''

Chapter Six

So much for making an early start. By the time Gale finally got to sleep, a pale sunrise was already beginning to silhouette the trees outside her window. As a consequence, she'd slept long past her usual rising time and wakened feeling stuffy and completely out of sorts.

She noticed it as soon as she threw back the covers: the bedroom was warm!

How could that be? She'd shut off the registers in all but the first-floor rooms of the main section of the house. Of course, a few of them, including the one in her bedroom, had been too stiff to close properly, but with the thermostat set at sixty-five, little if any heat leaked through.

Saxon must have gotten cold during his nocturnal wanderings and decided to do something more than just cut a little firewood for the study.

She'd just have to tell him about the bill, and offer him his choice of being a bit chilly for the duration of his visit, or warm as toast for a few days, and then, zap! Instant iceberg.

Gale knew these old granite mansions could be colder than Mount Mitchell in a blizzard. Saxon Hall would cool down pretty fast once all heat had been shut off. Grudgingly, she resigned herself to sleeping in a hat, socks, gloves and a coat until either Olivia or Tad Benton got back to straighten out this mess with the bank. She was beginning to feel like a first-class incompetent, when actually, it was the bank's mistake. *Forced Into A Life Of Crime By The Blue Ridge Savings Bank.* Perhaps her next book would be a detective thriller instead of another children's story.

There was no sign of Saxon when she pushed open the kitchen door, and Gale assured herself that she was relieved. She was determined to finish the Biltmore shoot in one trip, and that called for a clear head and a decent breakfast.

Having to face Saxon this morning would hardly have been conducive to either. At this point, Gale didn't know how she felt toward him—resentment at his having taken control of her thermostat, or embarrassment at his having taken control of her better judgment.

There was no doubt about it: Biltmore House, the 12,000-acre estate completed in 1895 by George Vanderbilt, had to be one of the finest homes ever built in the Americas. Westerly, the Chandlers' estate, would have been considered palatial by some standards. If a couple of small wings and the conservatory were lopped off, it would have fit comfortably in the Vanderbilts' banquet hall.

"Two-hundred and fifty-five rooms, boys—take your pick," she said cheerfully as she bent a couple of wires, snapping Golly's ears to attention and pointing his right paw toward the French Renaissance-style castle. "Just remember to wipe your feet before you go inside, okay?"

With only three locales left to shoot, Gale had deliberately chosen the one farthest from home. Of course, she might still have to go back and retake some of the more recent ones; since Sax's arrival, she'd been neglecting her darkroom work.

The darkroom could wait. Today, the sky was a deep shade of blue that made it a perfect foil for the few tiny clouds that drifted by like blobs of whipped cream. The air was so clear that sunlight glinted from the row of visitors' cars in front of the main entrance.

Which was one of the reasons she was where she was, instead of plopped down in the middle of the grounds proper, Gale reminded herself as she lined up the first shot of the pair of weary, travel-stained orphans, awed by what appeared to be the answer to all their dreams.

She framed the shot, with Biltmore House in the distance and the stuffed dog and rag doll in the foreground. After a moment's consideration, she shifted her position so that none of the large red oak leaves on the overhanging branch were visible. By trial and error, she'd discovered that a single misplaced leaf could throw a whole picture out of scale and ruin the illusion. She now carried with her an assortment of tiny leaves more in scale with her other props and a tube of

superglue in case of emergencies. Richard's boxwoods were developing quite a few bald spots.

A few hours later, her work completed, Gale
breathed a sigh of satisfaction and put away her camera gear. She unwired the toys and removed the eyes—
she'd hit upon the idea of using different eyes and
eyebrows, attached with Velcro backings, to alter the
expressions. Her cast could now register a variety of
emotions, making the photos that much more realistic.

Finally, she dug in her camera case for the snack
she'd brought along. Leaning back on the rocks still
warm from the sun, Gale munched her apple and tried
to remember exactly how many copies of *The Bridge
to Golly's House* she'd already promised in exchange
for trespassing privileges. Otis Pilky and the man with
the orchard—that was two. Miss Hudgins, whose
greenhouse was full of overgrown potted palms, made
three. There'd been a few more, and that wasn't
counting the couple who'd allowed her access to today's vantage point.

No two ways about it, she simply *had* to get the
story published. Her whole future, not to mention her
ego, hung on pulling it off in the face of the total lack
of support.

Today's goal had been to point up the contrast between Boy's grandiose dreams and Golly's more
practical ones by using Biltmore House as a foil for the
dilapidated cottage where Miss Vanilla, who was losing her sight and too proud to admit it, lived all alone.

Palaces were all very well, but they were no guarantee of happiness. Take Susan, for instance, Gale
mused, trying to ignore the cold that was beginning to

seep through the seat of her pants from the damp ground.

No, not Susan. Susan lived in a palazzo and was disgustingly happy at last report. Take Saxon—

Gale shifted position, suddenly aware that various portions of her anatomy were beginning to grow numb as the last of the day's warmth dissipated from the rocks.

Saxon Hall was no Biltmore House. It wasn't even a mansion like Westerly, but it was a gem of a house, and still considered a showplace. Yet Saxon didn't seem to have found much happiness there. Otherwise he'd never have stayed away so long.

Personally, Gale seldom gave much thought to happiness as such. At the moment, she'd willingly settle for a feeling of competence and independence. If she dared to dream at all, it was of being able to support herself with her typewriter, her camera and her imagination.

She was one day closer to that goal, she told herself as she trudged up the wooded slope to where she'd left her car. After a mental review of the day's work, she felt even more optimistic. Of the three rolls she'd taken, she'd probably use no more than two shots, but they'd be the *perfect* two. "Happy ending, here we come," she crowed as she carefully laid the Hefty bag on the back seat.

Less than five miles from home on Bear Cave Road, the narrow, winding shortcut she sometimes used when she traveled to and from Asheville, her car shuddered, sputtered and died. There was barely time enough for Gale to steer off onto the shoulder.

Barely enough shoulder to steer off onto, she amended a few moments later as she peered over a sheer drop of several hundred feet.

"Garage, nothing, I should have parked you in the utility room," she grumbled, sliding carefully back inside after a brief and pointless survey under the hood. If it had been a flat tire, she could have changed it, although she didn't relish the idea of using a bumper jack halfway between a narrow mountain road and the edge of the earth.

But it was nothing so simple as a flat tire. She hadn't a clue what could have stalled the car. Everything under the hood looked pretty much the way she remembered it from the last time she'd filled the windshield washer bag. Maybe she should have studied auto mechanics instead of taking all those art and creative writing courses. At least she'd know which tire to kick in an emergency.

It was slightly more than a mile back to the nearest farm. If there was no phone there, Gale told herself as she hiked along the narrow shoulder, at least she might find someone who had more than a nodding acquaintance with the internal combustion engine.

Luckily, there was a phone. While her stomach growled at the smell of corn bread and country ham that was just being set out for supper, she searched her purse to make certain she had enough money with her to pay for the call, and then looked up the number of Shepparton's only towing service.

"Fifty-five dollars!" she exclaimed a moment later. "forget it, I'll make other arrangements."

Disheartened, she hung up the phone and tried to summon a reassuring smile for the bustling woman who was opening a jar of homemade watermelon preserves. "No problem," she lied. "I have a friend who can probably—" Dialing as she spoke, she tapped a damp, frozen foot on the shining vinyl floor. "Sax? Thank goodness! Look, could you possibly bring the Jeep and a rope out to Bear Cave Road? It'll be the first turnoff past..."

She listened as Saxon assured her that he hadn't forgotten the back road where he'd learned to drive at age thirteen.

"Well, okay then. I'll be parked on your right about three miles after you leave the main highway." Thank heavens for her mustard-yellow car; at least it'd be easy to spot.

"I just hope he remembered to bring a rope," she muttered anxiously a half hour later. Sax had maneuvered a daring turn and pulled the Jeep off onto the shoulder just in front of her. She watched as he climbed out, looking more beautiful than any man had a right to look in faded jeans, scuffed boots and a battered leather jacket. She hoped he had on long johns too. The wind had dropped once the sun had disappeared, but so had the temperature.

Sax opened the door and slid in beside her, giving her barely enough time to scramble across to the passenger side. "I set out a couple of emergency blinkers, since yours don't seem to be working."

Gale tried to look competent and mechanical. Never having had to use them, she'd forgotten all about blinkers. She wasn't even sure she had any. "Thanks," she said coolly, and then caught her breath as a car had whizzed past, taking the hairpin curve so wide that she gripped the dashboard and waited to go sailing off into the tree tops below.

"From now on I'm sticking to the interstate if it takes me all day to get where I'm going. At least they have emergency lanes."

Saxon took a deep breath, unzipped his coat and looked around, as if to familiarize himself with his surroundings. Catching sight of the bulging Hefty bag, camera case, tripod and a couple of small reflectors in the back seat, he lifted one eyebrow, but refrained from comment. "Okay, first let's go over what happened," he said. "Has it ever died on you this way before?"

"Never."

"I take it this isn't a computerized model."

"I don't like digital watches. I actively hate computers."

"Hmm. That rules out one possibility. Let's rule out a few more. I'll take a look under the hood."

"Men *always* take a look under the hood," Gale muttered. "For your information, I've already looked."

"And?" Leaning his back against the door, he regarded her in a way that left her feeling slightly less intelligent than a rutabaga.

"I didn't have a flashlight." She burrowed her fists deeper into the pockets of her red windbreaker and stared at the damp patches on the knees of her yellow jeans. Her flashlight, of course, was still in the study where she'd left it last night. If he dared to bring that up, she *would* bop him!

He didn't. Instead, he turned on the ignition and studied the few gauges on the dashboard. Switching on the key, he experienced the same frustrating lack of response she had.

"I could have told you it wouldn't work."

He ignored her sarcasm. "I'd better take a look." Opening the door, he swung his legs out and then turned to glance at her over his shoulder. "You okay?"

Gale, who'd spent the usual amount of time on her knees, her bottom, and her stomach angling for the perfect shot, said airily, "Of course I'm okay. If you don't count freezing, starving and an incipient case of acrophobia."

Sax grinned. Peeling off his leather jacket, he handed it to her, still warm from his body. "I promise I'll feed you at the first opportunity, but first let's get this show off the road before another budding Indy 500 contender comes barreling around the bend."

Several minutes later, he slid in beside her again, chafing his hands together. "It gets cold out in the Oklahoma panhandle, but it gets *cold* in these mountains," he stressed. "Especially once the sun goes down. I'm no crack mechanic, but I couldn't find anything wrong. Gale, are you sure you didn't just run out of gas?"

Huddled guiltily in the warmth of his huge leather coat, Gale pointed to the gauge. "Half a tank. I filled her up just last week. Or was it the week before?" she added half under her breath. "No matter, the gauge says I have plenty of gas, so it can't be that. What about her battery?"

"Battery's all right, considering you damn near cranked it to death. You say you filled up two weeks ago? What sort of mileage do you get and how much driving have you done?"

"I'm not sure about the mileage. As for how much driving I do..." A lot, she thought uneasily. Enough so that she should have used up more than half a tank by now.

With growing suspicion, she leaned across Sax's knees and whammed the gauge with the side of her fist. To her horror, the needle slowly descended toward the empty tank. And kept going. "I don't believe this," she whispered. "She lied to me. After all the premium gas and high-grade motor oil I've bought her, all the times I've parked and walked over rough roads just to save her from having to endure ruts and rocks and mud, she *lied* to me."

Saxon said nothing. Instead, he gathered Gale against his side and covered her cold hands with one of his. Hers were chapped and cold, and none too clean; his was warm and callused, and smelled slightly of soap and motor oil. "Some women are like that," he murmured against her hair. "All the privileges, all the advantages, and still they deceive you. Beats all understanding, doesn't it?"

"I'm going to find this pretty hard to forgive." Gale was struggling not to succumb to the same sort of madness that had claimed her in the small hours of the night. It was an uphill battle.

"You might not be able to help yourself. Sometimes our emotions don't pay a hell of a lot of attention to our brains." Sax tucked her icy fingers under his arm, against the solid, flannel-clad warmth of his chest. While they tingled from restored circulation, he began slowly stroking the length of one of her corduroy-covered thighs.

The tingling spread. Gale wriggled closer. She was a little old to be making out in a parked car on a lonely mountain road. On the other hand, better late than never. Food could wait.

"Here comes another car." Sax removed his hand from her thigh and eased his arm from around her shoulder. "If you've thawed out enough to drive, I'll see if I can siphon some gas out of the Jeep. Your battery's going to get another workout trying to pump it into her system."

"She owes me."

"I just hope she doesn't get indigestion from the low octane." *Indigestion? Good Lord, she had him doing it again!*

"Serves her right if she does," Gale retorted. "What can I do to help?"

"Just sit tight and let me see if I've got everything I need. There's a pretty complete emergency kit in the back of the Jeep, everything from flares to space blankets. Want a foil wrapper to keep you warm? This might take awhile."

"No thanks, but you'd better take your coat before you go back out there. I'm beginning to thaw out, and I'd hate to have you catch pneumonia on account of my carelessness."

"Stop feeling guilty, it could've happened to anyone."

Gale slid over to the place he'd just vacated, ready to do whatever she could to help the cause. "Don't worry," she said with a rueful grin, "I can do without another dose of guilt. Promise you'll yell if I can hold a light or a can or anything."

By the time they got home, Gale was almost too tired to be hungry. Her face, hands and feet tingled painfully from the cozy warmth that greeted her when she walked into the kitchen, and she turned accusingly to Sax, who was hanging his coat over the back of a kitchen chair. "You left the heat on!"

He looked at her as if she'd suddenly accused him of treason.

"So?"

"So... Well, normally, I turn it down if I'm going out."

"Normally you don't even bother to turn it on at all," he said pointedly, making her wish she'd kept her mouth shut. She was too tired at the moment to get into all that, and besides, a miracle could still happen, and he'd never even have to know.

"It's only November," she said, busying herself with removing her coat and folding it neatly.

"Go wash up. I'll open a can of something and put it on to heat. Any suggestions?"

"Anything, just so long as it's fast. If it's soup, though, I can't promise I won't fall asleep with my face in the plate and drown."

"I'll stand by with a life preserver in case of an emergency," Sax promised with a smile that threatened to undermine the last vestige of her strength.

"She-crab soup, then—with lots of sherry," Gale suggested.

"If Mrs. McCrary's left us any." Sax opened a cabinet and rummaged among the cans.

"Brandy's her preference, but I notice the decanter's missing."

"I hid it. A lot of things seem to have turned up missing around here, but we won't go into that tonight."

Gale's spirits sank. Already at the door, she turned and leveled a resigned look at his extremely masculine backside. "If you're going to keep bringing it up, Sax, then let's *do* go into it tonight. Frankly, it's been eating holes in my conscience. I'd just as soon get it over with."

"Go wash up. We'll eat first."

Suddenly, she wasn't hungry any more. At the thought of having to tell Saxon about all the things she'd taken to Mr. Crump, her stomach tightened like a small, hard fist. Getting things out into the open was all for the best, she told herself. With someone to share the burden, it wouldn't seem so overwhelming. Besides, Sax could probably make Bahanian down at the bank listen to reason—he might even be able to unravel the whole silly mess, all the way back to where things had started getting crazy. All those overdue bills coming out of the woodwork—!

Several minutes later she presented herself back in the kitchen, clean, warm, and torn between hunger and apprehension. "Smells great," she observed with forced cheerfulness as she watched Sax divide the contents of a copper saucepan into two blue-glazed soup plates.

"Saxon, I don't think I ever got around to thanking you for coming to my rescue, but I really do appreciate it. I didn't know who else to call after I found out how much a tow truck charges to go out that far at this time of night."

Buttering a cracker with the precision of a surgeon, Sax nodded. "You're welcome."

Gale sighed and laid down her spoon. "Sax," she began, but he shook his head.

"Finish your soup first."

Finish her soup. Why did she have the feeling that she was partaking of the condemned criminal's last meal? Dutifully, she lifted her spoon and stirred a shred of crab meat around. She sighed.

She sighed again.

Sax swore softly and shoved back his chair. "All right, dammit, if you insist on getting it over with now, let's go on into the study!"

Perversely, now that the time had come, Gale found herself perfectly willing to put it off a little longer. Indefinitely, in fact. She took another spoonful of her soup and reached for another cracker, sending him an unconsciously pleading look as he hovered over her.

But Sax had had enough of waiting. He'd stewed for days, alternately wanting to throw her in jail for stripping bare the home that held whatever memories, good and bad, he had of his childhood, and wanting to throw her into his bed and make love to her until he got her out of his system. "I've had just about all I can take from you," he said in a tone that caused her to shrink against the back of her chair.

"Why don't I make us a pot of coffee?" she suggested brightly.

"To hell with coffee! If you're through, get a move on. I've wasted enough time, as it is—I'd like to get this over with."

"Not half as much as I would," she said miserably to his back as she reluctantly followed him through the swinging door, across the dining room, the foyer and along a short corridor to the study. His hard leather boot heels rang out sharply as he strode across the bare wooden floors. Her sneakers whispered apologetically as she trotted along behind him.

There was no fire glowing on the hearth. Somehow Gale didn't think it would have helped to defrost the atmosphere if there'd been a raging inferno in the room. Saxon's cold blue eyes would have extinguished it in a minute.

It was hard to believe that less than an hour ago, he'd lent her his coat and warmed her in his arms.

All at once, Gale decided that she was tired of being on the defensive. Swinging around to confront him, she said belligerently, "You know, Saxon, you really ought to give that Jekyll and Hyde act of yours a rest. You've got it down pat, but it's very confusing! I was actually beginning to believe we could be friends, and then it dawned on me that it's all just a game you play. A silly game you use to keep me off balance."

Sax's gaze bored into hers. Gale could almost swear he grew several inches in height. She flinched, but she refused to back down. "Well, for your information, I've *had* it with you blowing hot one minute and cold the next! I've changed my mind; I don't want to talk to you about anything. Ever!"

Dear Lord, did that really sound as childish as she thought it did? Righteous indignation was one thing, petulance quite another.

Sax narrowed his eyes. There was a small pulse showing in the open throat of his dark shirt, and Gale couldn't seem to tear her gaze away from it. "All finished?" he asked silkily.

She swallowed. Dropping her fists from her hips, she nodded warily. "Well, you are pretty unreasonable, you know," she said defensively. "It's as if there were two of you."

"And you prefer the one who—as you put it—blows hot?"

Saxon took a step closer.

Gale took a step back.

"No one enjoys getting her head bitten off for no reason at all," she declared.

"No reason?" He lifted his dark brow in surprise. Then he smiled and took another step, effectively trapping her between a sofa and table, unless she wished to make an undignified scramble for freedom over a pipe stand and a magazine rack. "All right, we'll let that pass for now," he conceded. Before she could tell what he had in mind, he was gripping her arms in a deceptively gentle hold. He smiled down at her as if she were a particularly succulent mouse and he were a circling hawk.

The match was lost before it even began. Sax was not above using the unfair advantage of size and strength, and once more Gale found herself in his arms, this time with the added threat of being in a warm, private place instead of on a public highway.

"Saxon, don't," she begged softly when his late-day stubble scraped against the tender skin of her face as he lowered his head to her lips. "Don't confuse me this way, please."

"Stop hiding from me, Gale. This is what you wanted, wasn't it? This is what you've been asking for?"

Indignantly, she threw back her head to glare at him, realizing too late the trap he'd set. "I never—!"

It was as far as she got. The sweet, wild taste of his mouth scattered all thought of resistance.

Chapter Seven

Slowly Saxon sank down onto the sofa, carrying Gale down on top of him. Tomorrow he'd be damning himself for being seven kinds of a fool, but tonight it just didn't seem important. With the evidence of his own eyes, plus the words of her beautiful mouth to condemn her, he still couldn't seem to keep a cool head when he was with her for any length of time.

A man could live a long time and still not uncover all his own weaknesses.

Sax twisted his fingers in the dark strands of tangled silk, pressing her head into the hollow of his throat. She smelled of sunshine and soap and warm woman. No wonder she thought he was playing games. God, if this was a game, then he was definitely the loser!

"Saxon, we were going to talk," Gale protested, and he tightened his arms at her words.

"No." His voice was soft, but implacable. He refused to argue with her. He didn't know what the hell she'd done to him, but he did know enough to shut up.

He could feel her trembling against him, feel the heat kindling between them. His hand moved hungrily over her back, brailling the delicate pattern of her ribs, following the shallow valley of her spine as it flowed down into the sweet delta of her hips.

Some ragged remnant of reason tried to hold out against the heavy pressure of his loins, arguing that he was making a grave mistake.

His senses won, hands down. She was so incredibly fragile! Like one of those small, gray-brown birds that fluttered around under the trees, always staying just out of reach.

God knows, he'd tried to explain it away, the crazy way she affected him. It was no good. No matter how many times he reminded himself that she'd barely waited for the door to close behind his family before she'd started stripping the place bare, it didn't seem to make any lasting impression. He had no idea what else she'd taken besides the rugs and the paintings, or what she'd done with the proceeds. At this moment, he didn't really give a damn.

One of his hands found its way under her sweater. It was like stroking cream. Lying on top of him, she wriggled to a more secure position, and he caught his breath and began desperately counting down from one hundred.

Think, man! Eighty-seven, eighty-six—this is your last chance to take charge of this situation!

All right, what about those two bulging bags she brings home every day. Tools? Loot? He hadn't missed the pliers and those scraps of wire on her dashboard, nor the coil of thin rope on the back seat.

But as he stroked the warm flesh of her back, brushed her hair aside to explore the vulnerable hollow of her nape and then spanned the delicate line of her throat, he remembered the way she'd looked that night they'd gone out to dinner, laughing across the table while the candlelight turned her eyes into amber witch stones.

If only he didn't keep getting these mixed signals!

What the devil had she been up to today? For that matter, what was she up to *every* day? Invariably she came home just before dark, looking as if she'd crawled backward through a storm drain or someone's dirty cellar window. Never a word about where she'd been, what she'd been doing—or what she carried in those bags she was seldom without.

The simple thing would have been to ask her, but crazy as it was, Sax had discovered that he really didn't want to know.

"Ah, Gale, why'd you have to do it?" The protest was forced from him. He squeezed his arms around her tightly, crushing her small breasts against the hard wall of his chest, and he found himself seeking excuses, wanting to protect her from her own weakness.

Gale ruffled his hair with her fingertips, savoring the different textures—the minklike softness of the dark brown, the vitality of the pewter.

Savoring everything about the man. He felt so right to her, as if he'd stepped into a hollow in her life that had been tailor-made to fit him.

But he was driving her crazy with these mood shifts. She knew she owed him an explanation; she just wished he'd make up his mind what he wanted from her. And in what order. "Sax, I know it was wrong," she admitted huskily, twisting one of the buttons on his shirt between her fingers. "Maybe I could have held off a little longer, but—" The button came undone, distracting her, and she shrugged, not an easy thing to do when you're lying prone on top of a large, tense man. "Well, to be perfectly honest, I was hoping you wouldn't have to find out."

"I think I understand, honey."

Beneath her, Gale could feel Sax inhale deeply. After a long moment, he exhaled in a heavy sigh, and she hung on and rode it out. She could almost read his thoughts. He was going to be *nice* to her. She'd stolen from the man, and he knew it, but he was going to be forbearing and understanding and forgiving. For as long as it suited him, at least.

The shameful thing was that it suited her, as well. If only they didn't have this—embarrassment—between them, there was nowhere she'd rather be than right where she was.

Only how the devil could he expect her to feel penitent when he was cupping her hips in his large, warm palms, and holding her against him this way?

Somebody had to take charge here, and it looked as if she was elected. "Sax, if we're going to talk about it, then maybe you'd better—that is, maybe I'd better get off. I mean, up."

"Now who's blowing hot and cold?" he teased. He framed her face in both hands, holding her there for a small eternity as he searched her eyes. His own were the deep, opaque blue of the mountains, and totally unreadable.

"You're the one who wanted to talk," she managed to whisper.

"Why don't we postpone this discussion of your transgressions to a later date, hmm?"

"First we're going to talk, then we're going to wait. Honestly, Sax, I'd just as soon get it off my chest. Maybe then I can stop feeling so guilty."

"First let's get you off my chest." He stood up, swinging her up into his arms without ever giving her a chance to escape. "Maybe you need to feel guilty a little longer to atone for your sins."

"I wouldn't exactly call it a sin," she protested weakly.

"Since when is stealing not a sin?" With one hand he switched off the light and strode toward the door.

Dear Lord, what now? Was he going to throw her out bodily, or was he planning on locking her up until he could get the sheriff to haul her off to jail?

"I'd prefer to call it borrowing." She'd prefer *he* thought of it as borrowing.

Sax chuckled, but Gale was not reassured. He didn't sound all that amused. "I'll just bet you would," he said. "And at the moment, I'm inclined to let you call it anything you want to." He headed up the stairs, carrying her in his arms as if she were as fragile and as precious as any of the porcelain pieces she'd ... borrowed.

"Saxon, I'm not sure we ought to be—"

Halfway up the stairs, he paused. In the dim light from the hall fixture, he looked shadowy and strange, not at all the man she'd had a crush on all those years ago and never quite managed to forget.

"To be what, Gale? Going upstairs together? I promise you, you can walk away from me any time you want to. I won't try to stop you."

Any time she wanted to, there was the hitch. Tremulously aware of dangers both real and implied, she said, "Then would you please put me down?"

Instead, he lowered his mouth to hers, closing in swiftly before she had a chance to escape.

As if she'd ever stood a chance of escaping.

The kiss began right there on the stairway, continued to the second floor, and on down the hallway, to the room she'd made up for him. It covered her lips, her cheeks, her eyelids and the vulnerable place on her temple, where his breath fanned her ear.

It carried her through the doorway, where he allowed her to slide down his body until her toes barely touched the floor. "Open your mouth, Gale," he commanded softly.

The warm sweep of his tongue made her knees buckle, and she sagged against him. He held her tightly, and half supporting, half leading, he carried her to his bed. Gale was no match for the hot, sweet tide of desire that washed over her. Sweeping away the minor obstacles of caution and wisdom, it left her utterly defenseless.

She drifted, steered by the needs of her own body, the demands of his. Conscience whispered that she might have held out a little longer if she'd tried harder, but in the end it would have been the same. Who was she to deny herself the fulfillment of a young girl's dreams and a woman's needs?

"Gale, stop thinking whatever you're thinking," Sax ordered with gruff tenderness. He was gazing down at her as she lay in his arms, tracing one finger around the delicate edge of her jaw until it reached her ear. "Your eyes are like windows. I told you you could walk away if you still had any doubts, and I meant it."

Fat chance, she thought helplessly. "I think I'll stay put," she told him.

"Maybe I should have asked first—am I treading on anyone else's territory? It's been a year, after all."

She shook her head. "Memories that might get in the way?" he persisted, and again she shook her head.

Gale didn't want to think about Jeff now, but maybe it bothered Sax. There'd been some sort of relationship between the two men, although she'd never heard either one of them refer to it. "Sax, there aren't any memories. No good ones, anyway. I'm sorry." For his sake, she meant.

"I'm glad," he said simply. Kneeling beside her, he stripped off his shirt and tossed it aside. Patches of color appeared high on his cheeks, sharpening the planes of his face. Tenderly, he brushed the hair back from her forehead.

Gale couldn't bring herself to ask if he had any memories, old or new, to come between them—any ties. There were enough problems to be worked out as it was; if there were more, she didn't want to know about them. Not just yet.

Sax's hands were none too steady as he removed her shoes and socks and slid off her pants. He pressed a kiss onto the warm place just below her waist, and she fell apart.

Quickly, he stood, unbuckled his belt, and stepped out of his jeans. Gale stared, mesmerized by the lean strength evident in every line of his body, from the hard, muscular thighs with their covering of dark hair, to the flat corded stretch of stomach that rose above his navy briefs, to the magnificent chest. In the light that spilled in from the hallway, he was the most beautiful man she'd ever seen.

Sax saw her gaze dart downward and then bounce back again, and he smiled. "Your turn," he challenged softly, indicating the silk undershirt she wore with her bikini panties. He'd already removed her sweater. Now he peeled off the last layer. One knee braced beside her on the bed, he stared down at what he'd uncovered, his gaze dwelling openly on the smallest of details.

And they were small, all right. Gale was acutely aware of the fact that when it came to physical endowments, she had a perfect set of teeth, and that was about all.

Her hands fluttered up to cover her breasts, and he captured them, kissing each palm in turn. Laughing softly, he drew her arms around his neck and lowered his face to kiss each soft, pink crest until it hardened under the sensuous caress of teeth, lips and tongue.

But the laughter had faded, the tension evident in every hard muscle of his body by the time he slid his hands under the elastic of her underpants to ease them down her legs. Gale drew her legs up in an instinctive gesture of defensiveness, and he kissed her knees, paying particular attention to a tiny pale crescent on the right one, a memento of her first attempt at ice skating.

"You have no reason to hide, love. You must know how beautiful you are." His voice was a deep, resonant whisper that did unbelievable things to her nervous system.

"Oh, I—" She met his eyes, drawn by the power and strength she'd always known he possessed. "I think I might be the least bit nervous," she confessed, and he smiled then, a slow, warm smile that poured over her like a benediction.

Gale knew in that single moment that she loved him. The crush that she'd carried buried within her for over a dozen years exploded into the deeper emotion—no matter what happened in the future, that one truth would remain.

She lifted her arms, and this time the kiss lasted a long, long time. They explored each other freely, joyfully, using all the senses, and a few that Gale had never even dreamed of, until finally, Saxon captured both her hands in one of his and held them over her head, tormenting her with a series of kisses that had her straining to escape.

"So aggressive for such a little girl," he teased.

"I might be small, but I'm no little girl." Her head twisted on the pillow as one of his fingers trailed circles around her breast, down over her soft stomach, to dip into the tiny indentation there.

"No, you aren't, are you?" His deep chuckle vibrated all through her body, and she tugged her hands free and captured his head, drawing him down so that she could claim his mouth once more.

"My fierce little dove," he whispered, and she nipped his bottom lip. He gave her his tongue, but it was no longer enough. She wanted all of him.

One of her hands strayed down his chest, toying with the whorls of crisp body hair until she found his nipple. He was so responsive! She'd never dreamed she could have such an effect on him.

Sax covered her breast with his hand as he plundered her mouth. In imitation of her own tentative attentions to his nipple, he circled, stroked and proceeded to drive her wild as he lavished attention on the small pink button.

His tongue swirled relentlessly, and she felt her thighs part in trembling anticipation. How could it be that he knew her needs even better than she did herself?

"Sax, please—I think I'm dying!" she gasped, writhing helplessly.

"Not just yet, little dove."

She took the hand that was cradling her breast and pushed it downward. "Sax, would you...touch me?" She could feel him smiling, and her face burned in the darkness. Never would she have believed that she could be so bold, so utterly wanton.

He moved his hand downward, grazing her stomach, settling fleetingly in the shallow cradle of her pelvis, finally brushing against the hidden valley. Throbbing with mindless need, she lifted her hips to meet his touch.

Deliverance. That was all she could think of now.

There was tension in every sinew of his body as she rose to meet him. Sax was stunned by the depths of passion he'd uncovered. She'd been married; he'd expected a certain level of experience, but he'd never expected this quicksilver responsiveness. By turns shy and aggressive, she'd proceeded to drive him to the very edge of reason, using a brand of sorcery he couldn't begin to comprehend.

Her needs were suddenly the most important thing in his world. She was so incredibly lovely in her pleasure and he wanted to be the one to give it to her.

Deliverance came in a blinding burst, but it was still not enough. Gale tugged at his shoulders, even while the bands of pleasure shimmered around her, drawing closer, nearly close enough to touch. She wanted all of him—she needed to be a part of him, to give him what he'd given her. She needed to fly again, and this time, not alone.

He came into her swiftly, filling her with a strength and power that was incredibly beautiful in itself. For one blinding moment, Gale knew what it was to be truly a part of another human being. Never before had she known such closeness, not even in the early days of her marriage.

And then she was beyond all knowing. Slow, powerful strokes built the tension, gathering it tighter and tighter around her, until she felt herself leaving earth once more. A voice kept repeating a single word. Her voice. His name.

Faster, higher, out of control they flew, clinging together for one long, incandescent moment.

Sax whispered her name hoarsely as they drifted down again slowly, turning on the wind like a feather caught in small eddies of lingering pleasure.

Breathing heavily, both were drenched in sweat. Neither of them knew or cared. Gale kissed the part nearest her, which happened to be the base of his throat, savoring the salty taste of him.

"I'm crushing you—why didn't you say something?" Sax adjusted his weight, drawing her tightly into his arms, where she curled contentedly against him.

"I didn't think I could talk. I'm still not sure which parts of me are functioning and which aren't."

"If you want an accounting as of about three minutes ago," he said with a soft chuckle, "I might be able to help you out."

"Mmm, maybe later," she murmured sleepily.

He tightened his arms around her. With her cheek resting in the warm hollow between his neck and his shoulder, she felt secure and loved, and more than willing to put off until tomorrow the things she should have done today.

Tomorrow came by degrees. The first degree was the realization that she was not in her own bed. Harder mattress. Fewer covers.

No nightgown!

The second degree of knowledge came when she squinted one eye open and saw in the dusky light a familiar-looking shirt hanging on a doorknob.

The remaining degrees followed rapidly, and Gale groaned and sat up in bed, dragging a corner of the sheet up to cover her. Being essentially a morning person, she was able to assimilate the few facts and put them into perspective without too much trouble.

Fact number one was that she was in love with Sax. Fact number two—she'd *made* love with him.

Fact number three was that he seemed to have disappeared.

What now? Should she lounge around looking seductive and wait for him to make the next move, or attend to business as usual? If she'd thought for one minute that Sax's next move would include coffee, she might have stuck it out a little longer, but something told her she'd have had a long wait.

Some forty-five minutes later Gale was showered, dressed with considerably more care than usual, and peering into the door of the garage. After several moments she turned away, frowning slightly. There'd been no note, no sign that he'd even made himself a cup of instant coffee. And the Jeep was gone.

Two hours later she was still procrastinating. It was another perfect day; she could have been all set up by now to finish shooting Golly's next scene. But then, if Sax should come back home or call, she'd miss him.

Besides, she rationalized, she'd neglected her darkroom work shamefully for the past week. There was printing to be done, and developing—contact proofs to be made and checked over. If she was going to have to reshoot anything, it would be better to know about it now, before the season changed too noticeably. An unexpected snowstorm could really mess up her continuity.

The call came shortly after noon, and Gale raced up the basement stairs, barely giving a thought to the prints floating in the tray of fixer. She could always print more.

"Gale, I'm at Medical Park General in Asheville," Sax said with no preamble. "Something's happened to Dad."

The next three days had no boundaries. After the first day, Sax booked a room at a nearby motel, and they took turns staying with Richard.

The first night they'd both stayed at the hospital. Gale had gone immediately at Sax's call. He'd been there since early that morning, having received a call from Laurel Hill just after five.

Richard had pulled loose his feeding tube. It was the first sign of movement in two months, and he'd been taken immediately to the hospital, where they could more easily monitor what was happening to him.

Throughout an endless day and into the following night, Gale had stood quietly by and watched as the man she loved grew more and more withdrawn. He'd said little as they waited. There'd been tests to be done, examinations by a whole battery of specialists. Nursing procedures had taken precedence over the needs of the family. As time wore on, they'd managed to hear odd bits and pieces of information that meant nothing at all out of context.

Neither one of them was good at waiting. Sax paced. Gale chewed her nails. She chafed at not knowing what was going on, at not even knowing whether to be hopeful or fearful.

No news is good news, she tried to tell herself. Fortunately, she had sense enough not to give voice to the platitude.

"Have you eaten anything at all today?" she asked the gray-faced man beside her once, and he stared at her as if she were a total stranger.

"I'm not hungry," he said.

Nevertheless, when Richard's doctor was finally able to offer them guarded reassurance, Gale insisted that Sax leave the hospital with her for an hour.

"You're not going to last another day at this rate. Richard's going to want to see you as soon as things calm down. What am I supposed to tell him—that you're conked out in the intensive care unit suffering from malnutrition, exhaustion and caffeine poisoning?"

A bowl of chili, a salad and a glass of milk was the best she could prepare in the allotted time. She tried to convince herself that his color was better, that his eyes didn't look quite so hollow.

"Feel better?" she asked gently.

It was as if he'd forgotten she was even there. "Hmm? Oh, yeah, sure. Thanks."

Gale sighed and fished the keys from her purse to drive them back to the hospital. If she'd had any lingering doubts about the depth of her feelings for this man, they were gone now. She'd gladly have spent the rest of her life doing whatever it took to make him happy. The fact that he might not love her no longer seemed relevant. What choice did she have? What choice did love ever give?

Later that day she drove home and brought back a change of clothes for them both. On the way out, she collected the mail that had accumulated, glancing through it automatically. Bills. A catalog—more bills. A letter for Saxon from some law firm in Oklahoma, but still nothing from Olivia.

Had anyone even thought to notify Olivia? Did anyone know how? All Gale knew was the name of the cruise line—she had it written down somewhere. Olivia was supposed to let Gale know how to reach her in case of emergency once she was on the ship. The arrangement had been, "Don't call me, I'll call you," which had suited Gale just fine. At the time.

"Saxon, have you managed to get in touch with Olivia?" she asked breathlessly the minute she got back. "The nursing home was supposed to call me if anything came up—I've been acting in her place while she's been gone. Oh, this is awful! I should have called before now, but I kept thinking I'd hear from her any day. She said she'd let me know when and where I could reach her."

"I wouldn't worry too much about it, Gale. Any wife who goes off and leaves her husband under these circumstances can't be all that concerned."

Guilt-ridden by the fact that she'd been relieved to see her mother-in-law leave, Gale felt compelled to defend her. "Don't judge her too harshly, Sax. I'm not sure Olivia was very strong even before Jeff's accident. Richard's stroke was just too much for her."

Saxon gave her a long, curious look. "All right, Gale. I'll withhold judgment. Give me the name of her ship, and when I have time I'll get a marine operator to track her down."

That night, after another guardedly reassuring conference with the physician, Gale persuaded Saxon to go to the motel and get a decent night's sleep. "I'll take the first shift, and you can relieve me whenever you feel like it."

"Promise you'll call me if there's the slightest hint of any change?" He was gray with exhaustion, and so hollow-eyed that it was all she could do not to gather him into her arms right there in the hall. The hospital staff was used to seeing displays of emotion, but she didn't think Saxon would appreciate it.

Time on, time off. They developed a fairly efficient pattern. Whoever was at the hospital would call before leaving, the call serving as a wake-up signal for the other.

They actually saw very little of each other. Gale sacrificed some of her sleeping time to dash back to the house in Shepparton and pack more clothes for both of them, leaving the soiled ones for Mrs. McCrary to launder. It pleased her inordinately to fold Saxon's clothing away in a drawer in the motel room and sleep in the bed he'd just vacated. She carefully rumpled her own bed each time, so that he wouldn't suspect she'd slept in his.

They could've taken two rooms, of course—if Sax had thought about it, he probably would have done so. Somehow, it hadn't seemed important. Neither of them had been thinking too clearly, and Gale treasured whatever small intimacies the situation provided.

Inevitably, there came a night when exhaustion caught up with both of them. It had been six days since Richard had been taken by ambulance from Laurel Hill to the hospital in Asheville. It had been a week of waiting for some further change, some indication of the extent of permanent damage. Gale had left the hospital shortly after Sax had slipped into the room. She'd been watching closely, along with the private-duty nurse, and was almost positive she'd seen some movement in one of his feet.

"Watch his toes," she'd whispered. "By the way, this is Agatha Crews—she's taking over this shift for the other nurse. Agatha, this is Mr. Evanshaw's son, Saxon."

The nurse, a plump, brown-haired woman with remarkably kind eyes, had nodded briefly and turned her attention back to monitoring her patient's blood pressure. It had been slightly elevated earlier, causing some concern. "Things are pretty quiet at the moment." She'd glanced back at Gale, and her expression had softened. "Now, promise me you'll eat a big supper and then take a good, brisk walk. I told them at the desk to let you have something for that headache. No point in wearing yourself to a frazzle."

So Gale had gone, and Saxon had stayed, with scarcely a word spoken between them. It was easier now that they had the system down pat; nevertheless, she missed those first few days when they'd both stayed up until they were ready to drop. It had been closeness of a sort, even if Saxon had seemed largely unaware of her presence.

She hadn't been able to sleep, in spite of an extravagant dinner in a good restaurant, the prescribed brisk

walk—eight times around the well-lighted complex—
and a rather dull television movie.

Her headache had subsided without the use of
medication, but she was still tense. Moments after deliberately relaxing every muscle in her body, she could
feel the tension gathering all over again at the back of
her neck and in her shoulders.

A massage from that wonderful physiotherapist out
at Laurel Hill would have done the trick. Barring that,
she chose the next best thing.

When she first thought she heard something, she
was in the bathroom, floating in a sea of bubbles that
had taken half a bottle of shampoo to achieve.
Through the open bathroom door came the soft
strains of some innocuous music, deliberately chosen
for its soporific effect.

"Gale?"

"Saxon?" Her yank at the shower curtain only
succeeded in jamming the rings.

"I thought you'd be asleep by now." She heard the
thud of a boot dropping, then another one. "Headache still bothering you?"

"Is Richard all right?" she called softly, ignoring
his question.

There was a pause, and Gale wondered whether to
lunge for the door or stay decently covered with bubbles except for her head, her shoulders and her feet.

"Yeah, he's doing fine. Blood pressure down,
everything looking good." When he spoke again, it
was from just outside the bathroom door. There was
the sound of running water, the clink of a glass, and
he said, "I caught your headache. Thanks a lot."

And then he was leaning in the doorway, gazing down at her, and there wasn't a thing she could do but stare back.

Chapter Eight

There was something in Sax's attitude as he gazed down at her, an odd sort of stillness, that left Gale powerless to protest. Neither of them moved for what seemed an eternity, and then Sax tossed back two small white tablets and reached behind him for a glass of water, draining the contents swiftly.

His gaze returned to the bathtub, but the frozen tableau had been shattered. The draft from the open door seemed to have disturbed the delicate ratio of bubbles to bathwater, leaving Gale increasingly exposed.

"How about closing the bathroom door on the way out?"

Saxon ignored her. He was almost afraid to move. The migraine was probably too far gone for the pills to touch it now—the blind spots and light flashes had started just after he'd left the hospital. For a little while he'd been afraid he wouldn't make it back to the motel without having to pull over and call for Gale to come get him.

Abruptly, he turned away, searching for the source of the dinning noise in the background. That damned radio on the bedside table—! How the hell did you turn the thing off?

Unable to focus his eyes on the infinitesimal white-on-black labels, he slapped at the row of buttons and succeeded only in knocking a glass ashtray to the floor. The noise continued unabated.

"Saxon, are you all right?" Gale called out.

The sound of water gurgling down a drain took on Niagaralike dimensions inside Sax's head, and he ignored her. He sprawled across the bed, closing his eyes to the glaring lights and trying to close his ears to the incessant whine of the saccharine music.

Gale found him that way a few minutes later as, still damp from her bath, she clutched the bath towel around her and poked her head around the door she'd slammed shut the minute she'd climbed out of the tub. "Oh, Saxon," she whispered, recognizing pain and exhaustion in every line of his body.

Taking just long enough to put on her nightgown first, she switched off the radio and all the lights except for the one in the bathroom, then closed the door halfway so that the glare cut only a thin slice across the teal blue carpet. Then she studied the large man lying crossways on top of the quilted counterpane. He'd managed to take off his boots before he collapsed, but he was still wearing that heavy leather jacket.

Quickly she began rolling up the heavy spread until it lay in a flat roll alongside his body. Next, she did the same with the blanket and top sheet. Somehow, she'd have to flop him over onto the sheet, and he was just going to have to cooperate. But maybe she'd better try to take off his jacket first.

Tugging gently on one sleeve at a time, she worked the stiff garment down his arms until she could free first one arm, then the other. Sax mumbled something vaguely threatening, but he didn't fight her. Tossing the jacket aside, Gale slid both her hands under one of his shoulders and tried to turn him. She'd worry about getting the rest of his clothes off once he was properly between the covers.

"Sax, you're going to have to help me," she whispered.

Again he groaned, but he obediently rolled over onto the smooth, cool sheets. Lying on his back, he covered his eyes with one arm. His face was pale and lined with exhaustion.

Keeping her touch as light as possible, Gale unbuttoned his shirt, unbuckled his belt and unzipped his pants. Then, kneeling beside him on the bed, she considered her next step.

The shirt could stay, she decided. There was no way she could get it off without a lot more manhandling, and she had an idea that the less of that he had to put up with, the better. He'd sleep well enough minus his jacket, boots and jeans. That is, he would if she could just get his pants off him and then aim him the right way. He was a little too long to sleep sideways in the bed and be comfortable.

First things first. Lips pursed and eyes primly averted, Gale tugged gently at his pant legs telling herself as she slid them down his legs, shook them out and folded them carefully over the back of a chair, that it was purely a matter of TLC. With the emphasis on *tender*.

Somehow she managed to get him properly aligned in the bed without too much difficulty. He immediately rolled over onto his side, facing the wall, and she dragged the heavy quilted counterpane off onto the floor and gently pulled the sheet and blanket up over his shoulders.

She watched him from the other bed. As her eyes grew adjusted to the darkness, she could see his shape under the pale blue bedding. He was lying on his right side, with his right leg extended, his left one drawn up. From the way his shoulders were hunched, his arms seemed to be crossed over his chest. His head was a dark shadow on the pillow, and Gale fancied she could see the tension gathering in his deltoids, constricting the flow of blood and aggravating his headache.

Come to think of it, her own shoulder muscles were like granite. No matter how many times she deliberately forced herself to relax, the tension crept back within minutes. Was that the way it was with Sax? Was he as cold as he looked? All locked up inside himself, with pain and anxiety his only companions?

Without pausing to think, Gale eased herself out of bed and crossed the carpeted space that separated the two large beds. Carefully, she lifted the edge of the covers and slipped in behind him, not quite touching him, but letting him feel her warmth.

If he needed it. If he wanted it, she told herself. He could just ignore her if it suited him, but if he needed her in the night, she'd be here within easy reach.

* * *

The radio blared out, eliciting a loud groan of protest from Sax, and bringing Gale upright beside him. "What on earth?" she exclaimed.

"Sorry—my fault." Sax rolled over onto his back. "I hit the damned thing last night trying to turn it off—must have accidentally set the alarm."

He hadn't stirred throughout the whole night as far as she could tell, and she'd been awake during most of it. Awake and aching to snuggle up against that solid sleeping form and wrap her arms around him, comforting him with her love. "Does that thing really say 10:10? It's a good thing somebody set something, or we'd have both slept until noon."

Sax sat up and stretched. Wearing nothing but a rumpled white shirt and a pair of navy briefs, with a heavy stubble darkening the lower half of his face and the aftermath of a migraine still shadowing his eyes, he should have looked dreadful. Instead, he looked wonderful.

Gale wished she'd had the foresight to return to her own bed sometime during the night. It hadn't occurred to her how her presence in his bed might look in the harsh light of day. In fact, she wished she'd had the foresight to sneak into the bathroom and wash her face, brush her hair, have it styled and trimmed and possibly undergo a little cosmetic surgery elsewhere. While she was at it, she might as well include a couple of silicone implants.

"Why don't I order us a pot of coffee and whatever else looks good?" Sax suggested.

"You feel like eating?"

"Don't you?" Sitting up in bed beside her, he drew up his knees and crammed a pillow behind his back.

Chummy. There was no other way to describe the grin
he gave her.

Thank goodness she was wearing her plainest flannel nightgown. At least he couldn't accuse her of
trying to look seductive.

While Sax ordered breakfast, Gale finished up in the
bathroom, acutely conscious every minute of the in-
timacy of the situation. While he shaved and showered, she called the hospital and was told that Richard
had rested comfortably and was doing as well as could
be expected.

"Standard message number three," she told him,
trying for breeziness. She repeated the mildly reassuring cliché and stepped into the closet to tuck her shirt-
tail into her slacks.

"I made the night nurse promise to let me know if
there was the slightest change," Sax said through the
closed bathroom door, and Gale stepped out of the
closet, refastening her narrow snakeskin belt. "Sax,
you know we could've eaten breakfast on the way to
the hospital." She searched for her purse and found it
under the shirt he'd discarded before he'd gone in to
shower and shave.

She buried her face in the rumpled fabric, inhaling
the scent of his body for one intoxicating moment. She
must have been out of her mind to agree to a setup like
this! Oh, the room was spacious enough. And it would
have been foolish for Gale to have insisted on her own,
especially since she couldn't afford to pay for it. Even
so, separate rooms might have been wiser.

In separate motels.

On opposite sides of town!

Sighing, Gale examined her neat beige slacks and
yellow oxford-cloth shirt in the mirror, finding them

suitably conservative. She tied her hair back with a scarf and slathered on a film of moisturizer.

Sax emerged from the bathroom, buttoning the cuffs of a clean white shirt. "I'm thinking of driving back home this morning and letting you go on to the hospital alone. I need to make a few calls, and that seems the easiest place to do it."

"That reminds me—there's a letter for you in the stack I picked up yesterday. I forgot to mention it."

Edging past him, Gale leaned toward the mirror to apply a light coat of gloss to her lips while he reached for the small stack and began shuffling through it. This was as good a way as any, she decided, for him to find out about all those bills. Goodness knows, she'd tried to confide in him, but every time either of them touched on the subject, something happened. They always seemed to get sidetracked.

She capped the lip gloss and dropped it into her purse. "Find it?"

He obviously had. He was frowning slightly, and Gale watched with undisguised curiosity as he ripped open the envelope. The return address listed a firm of lawyers in Guymon, Oklahoma. There could be any number of reasons for a man to be hearing from a law firm. It didn't have to be bad news.

Sax scanned the two pages and swore softly under his breath. Dammit, he should have called her. He'd been putting it off until he had some idea of when he'd be able to return to the ranch, and now she'd taken matters into her own hands. It wasn't the first time Enid had taken the initiative; she was not a patient lady.

"Problems?" Gale asked. She was eaten alive with curiosity and doing her best not to show it.

"Yeah, you might say."

She waited in vain for enlightenment. Sax took out his wallet and moved a couple of bills, and right on cue there was a knock on their door.

"Breakfast is served," he announced, changing the subject before she could think of a polite way to pry a little more information from him. The strong, silent type could be a real pain, Gale decided, dumping the silverware out of her rolled napkin and snapping the white linen square open across her lap.

Later that morning, when Sax rejoined her at the hospital she told him they were talking about moving his father back to Laurel Hill in the morning. "He's stabilized to the point where the staff there can handle things, and with this flu epidemic filling up all the beds, Dr. Pauley thinks he'll be better off in a smaller, more restricted situation."

"Probably for the best." Saxon agreed. "I guess this means we can move back home, then."

Gale shot him a covert glance. "It'll be good to get back to normal," she conceded. Safer, she meant. Sharing a motel room had been possible only because of the circumstances. It had worked for nearly a week, because they'd never been there at the same time. Until last night.

"Yeah," he said, leaving her completely in the dark as to his feelings on the topic.

"Yeah," she echoed, nodding morosely. "I'll be glad to sleep in my own bed again. At home, I mean," she added hurriedly, making things infinitely worse.

Sax's slow, teasing smile went a long way toward relieving any awkwardness she might have felt.

When they'd left the motel that morning, Sax had taken her keys, unlocked her car door and opened it.

"Got your room key?" he'd asked, and she'd nodded. "Lunch money?"

"Yep." She managed a cheeky grin, but meeting the intense flame of his eyes, she'd been unable to sustain it.

"Then I guess I'll be seeing you sometime early this afternoon. Meanwhile, if anything comes up, you know how to reach me."

Sax had continued to gaze down at her, holding her door open even after she'd slid into the driver's seat. Then, almost as if drawn against his will, he'd leaned closer, until his face eclipsed the slice of sapphire sky showing above the tops of the tall spruce pines.

He'd kissed her. A simple brush of the lips, with only a hint of lingering pressure, the kiss had wiped out all thoughts of why they were there, of what was to be done and of all that remained unsettled between them.

"Thanks for last night, little dove," he'd whispered, drawing back and carefully closing her door.

Gale had driven the entire distance to the hospital oblivious to the crush of rush-hour traffic that surged along on all sides.

Richard was moved on Sunday morning, and Gale and Sax followed the ambulance from the hospital to the skilled-care nursing home that was located halfway between Asheville and Shepparton. After seeing him settled into his old room, looking better than he had at any time since his stroke, they strolled back out to the beautifully landscaped parking area.

"I feel as if I've been gone for at least a month," Gale said. "I'd better pick up something for dinner on the way home."

Sax leaned up against the hood of her car, arms crossed over his chest, and stared at a circling hawk. "Gale, I don't know exactly how to tell you this, but, ah . . . we're having a houseguest for Thanksgiving."

"We're having a what?"

"I'm afraid the letter I got yesterday was from a friend—"

"You said a houseguest," Gale reproved. What kind of friend would invite himself to visit under these circumstances? Surely Sax could have put him off.

"I could always call and—"

"Don't even think about it," she snapped. Then, relenting, she laid a hand on his arm. "Sax, I'm sorry. The truth is, I'd forgotten all about Thanksgiving. I haven't seen a paper in days, or I'd have probably noticed all the turkeys and pilgrims."

"We can make reservations at the club for dinner, but she'll probably expect us to put her up at the house."

She? His guest was a woman? Gale's small store of generosity began withering away again. What sort of woman would invite herself to visit a man in his home?

Or had he invited her? For protection, perhaps? To let Gale know that he had other commitments?

She was probably being overly suspicious, she told herself. Meanwhile, if she was going to have to play hostess to one of his women, then she'd damned well do it up right!

Monday morning, with Mrs. McCrary's grudging cooperation, Gale opened up another of the second-floor bedrooms. That afternoon, with heavy rains in the forecast, she cut the last of the chrysanthemums and left them in a bucket in the utility room for arranging later. If they were a bit past their prime, that was hardly her fault. Sax could always order flowers if he wasn't satisfied with her efforts.

All her props and camera gear were right where she'd left them the night she'd gotten back from Biltmore, Gale noted guiltily. She hadn't had time even to think about her own work, but the minute she found a free moment, she was going to have to get back to it.

At the moment, her mind was filled with all the things that needed doing before Sax's girlfriend arrived on Wednesday. It occurred to her for the first time that he'd announced her pending visit shortly after receiving that letter from the law firm in Oklahoma. Could the lady be a lawyer?

Oh, great! That was just what she needed to make her feel really secure. How about a woman sheriff? Maybe he knew a few female police officers he could invite over for tea!

Gale made a deliberate effort to lower her blood pressure. Regardless of the circumstances, she needed to keep her wits about her. Besides, as hostess she owed it to Sax and any friend he cared to invite to be hospitable if it killed her.

The place was a mess, with Gale's having been gone for a week and Mrs. McCrary on her preholiday schedule. The housekeeper tended to start tapering her efforts a week or so before any federal holiday. It was probably too late to get anyone in to help with the floor, but if she could just find out which cleaner Olivia had sent the rugs to, maybe she could retrieve at least a couple of them to brighten up the main rooms.

She'd searched the kitchen desk earlier for a clue and found none, but Olivia had a desk in her sitting room upstairs. She might have stuck the receipt in that. She'd need to look into it right away though, before the cleaners shut down for the holiday.

She was bent over the little French provincial desk several minutes later when something made her pause in her efforts at getting it open and glance toward the door.

"What the hell are you doing to my mother's desk?" Sax thundered.

Gale cringed. "Your mother's desk? Oh. I didn't realize—well, of course, I should have—I mean, Olivia—"

"Gale," he said in an ominously quiet tone.

"I couldn't find the key, and I need to look for something." So the dainty little desk had belonged to his mother. Along with a lot of other things here, she supposed. No wonder he felt a bit resentful, but was that any reason to take it out on her?

Sax's eyes narrowed on the small figure clutching a nail file. "Well, I couldn't find the key," Gale said defensively. Try to do someone a favor, and this was the thanks you got!

"Exactly what is it you're looking for, if you don't mind my asking?" He didn't look particularly appreciative at the moment.

"I thought we might get a few of the rugs back for your company. The floors look so naked."

"The rugs?" There was no mistaking his look of surprise.

What the devil had he thought she was after, the crown jewels? "Well, they *do* look naked. The walls, too, but I doubt if we can get the paintings back in time. Anyway," she said with perverse satisfaction, "the rugs will cost a small fortune, and you're going to have to pay for it, because I just don't have that kind of money."

Sax turned to the window. Bracing a fist on either side of the frame, he stared out at the dense row of evergreens that surrounded the house. He swore softly. "I just don't believe this."

"Look, if you don't care what sort of impression your home makes on your friends, why should I? I only thought it would be nice to see things looking festive again—and I never cared to talk to a person's back."

With exaggerated patience, Sax turned, hooking his thumbs in the low waist of his jeans. The look he sent her could only be described as scathing. "Pardon me all to hell and back, Mrs. Evanshaw. Don't let me keep you from your lock busting."

Gale flinched as though she'd been struck, but her gaze never wavered. Carefully, she laid the nail file down on a polished fruitwood table. "I was only trying to help," she said carefully.

"You're not helping, Gale."

Pride and dishonesty. Had any man ever been confronted with such a baffling woman? Caught in the act, and she could still almost manage to convince him that he was the guilty party. Sax told himself that he was a rational man. From the very first night, he'd had the evidence of his own eyes. She'd confessed, and now he'd caught her in the act. How *could* she be innocent? There was no arguing with facts.

For the rest of that day, they took great pains to avoid each other. Sax drove back to Laurel Hill and stayed until long after dark. Gale dawdled over whether or not to fix dinner, finally making herself a sandwich, which she left untouched on the kitchen table. After awhile she went down to the darkroom and tried to concentrate on work, but somehow the excitement of blending illusion and reality failed to capture her imagination.

Then it was Tuesday. A guarded truce seemed to have evolved between Gale and Sax. Three days' notice, she thought with rancor as he sauntered into the kitchen. She was up to her elbows in cookbooks, having ruined one batch of cranberry relish and burned two piecrusts.

"Gale, I feel rotten about this." Sax stared around him at the floury chaos. After what had happened yesterday, he wouldn't have been surprised to discover she'd moved out and left him to the tender mercies of that brandy-swilling housekeeper. "I didn't want you to go to all this trouble. Enid would understand. With Dad just out of the hospital, it's unreasonable to expect anyone to throw a house party."

Enid. That sounded like a lawyer's name. Cool, austere, precise. "I don't mind, Sax. It's probably better for both of us to have something to keep our minds off Richard." To keep their minds off the way they continually struck sparks off each other, too. "Dr. Pauley said any progress would be slow, and we'd just have to be patient. I've discovered I'm not much good at being patient."

Lean hips braced against the edge of a counter, Sax frowned absently at the small creature wearing a flamingo print sweatshirt and yellow bunny slippers. That was the way she'd been dressed that first night when she'd opened the door to him.

How was it possible for any woman to scramble his brain to the point where he couldn't tell right from wrong—didn't even want to?

He'd come here with a single goal: to see his father and, if possible, make some sort of peace with him after eleven years. He'd known it wasn't going to be easy. What he hadn't counted on was finding his father's wife off on a pleasure cruise, his stepbrother dead and this bewitching little enigma installed in his home, by turns caring for his father as if he were her own, and robbing him blind.

What the hell was a man to think? What was he supposed to do? Ignore her misdeeds and hope he could keep her out of trouble?

Gale brushed the back of her wrist over her forehead, smearing it with a streak of flour. "How long is this friend of yours planning to stay, if that's not an indelicate question?"

"I don't have the slightest idea. According to her letter, she's on her way to visit a relative in Richmond, and as Shepparton's practically right on the way, she thought it would make a convenient break in her trip."

Gale snorted. She was beginning to suspect that Enid's visit was not as casual as it seemed. If she felt free to invite herself for the holiday, there was probably more than a professional relationship involved here. "Is she your lawyer, or what?"

"Enid? My lawyer?" Sax threw back his head and laughed, and Gale yanked open a cabinet door and scrambled noisily among the contents until she located two more pie tins. These she slammed down on the counter, sending up billowing clouds of flour.

"Look, I told you I could make reservations at the club," he reminded her. "It's still not too late." It was hard to realize that less than a month ago he'd actually toyed with the idea of asking Enid to marry him.

Now all he wanted to do was to send her on her way so that he could come to terms with all that had happened between him and Gale.

At the moment they seemed to have locked horns again, although damned if he could figure out why. For eyes as clear as a mountain stream, hers sure didn't give away much.

"Gale," he ventured, "shall I go ahead and make those reservations for Thursday?"

Glaring down at her floury fists, Gale said, "Saxon, if I want to cook Thanksgiving dinner, why should you complain? I haven't poisoned you yet, have I?"

"Now, honey—"

"Don't you 'now honey' me!"

He should have kept his distance until she'd had time to cool off. All things considered, it had been a lousy week. At the rate things were deteriorating, neither of them would last through the weekend.

"Would you mind moving so I can get to the oven?" Gale asked in an excessively polite voice. She was behaving abominably and she knew it. She just didn't know how to make herself stop.

"What are you doing—trying out for the role of lady of the house?" Sax's smile was not particularly pleasant. "But then, you've already got it, haven't you? With all the trimmings, as they say."

Gale spun around. Her eyes, large to begin with, looked enormous as the last vestige of color fled her face. "On second thought, why ruin a perfectly good turkey? If you call the club now, you can probably still get a reservation. I'll just clean up this mess and—and..."

The tip of her nose turned pink, and Sax could see at a glance that her chin was threatening to crumple.

Oh, God, why hadn't he just hit her while he was at it?
"Honey, I—"

"Mrs. McCrary would be glad to have the turkey,
if you don't mind my offering it to her. She had family coming—that's why she can't be here tomorrow."

"Gale, I—"

"Oh, and there was a call for you from a Mr. Trent.
He said he'd call back later this afternoon, something
about watching a game."

Sax closed his eyes momentarily in defeat. Out of
sheer frustration, he'd lashed out, cutting her to the
quick. Something told him she wouldn't easily allow
him to get close enough to make it up to her, either.

"Gale, would you just let me explain?"

"Explain what? I got carried away, that's all. Look,
if you don't mind, I have a few errands to run this afternoon. The yellow room's all in order, and I've got
enough flowers for the dining room and one more arrangement. Would she like them in the bedroom, do
you think?"

"Gale, dammit, *listen* to me!"

But she rushed on, eyes feverishly bright as she
swept piles of flour off the counter into a paper bag,
and began cramming utensils into the dishwasher.
"Some people don't like the scent of mums, especially not in a bedroom, but I think they're a lot
fresher smelling than lilies and tuberoses...."

Her voice trailed off as she stared at the door
swinging shut. He'd stalked off. Probably still mad at
her for trying to take over his home. It was no wonder he resented her being here. Olivia, too. Imagine
coming home after all these years only to find two
strange women installed in his house, with all his

mother's things. The holiday had probably just made it worse, intensifying his sadness and frustration.

At the moment, however, there wasn't one blessed thing she could do about it, except try to be a little more understanding.

And try to forget what had happened that night more than a week ago when he'd reached out to her, and she'd taken him into her heart and into her body.

"Just stop it this minute, Gale Chandler!" She'd never been a weeper. She wasn't about to start now, although surveying the mess she'd made in Saxon's kitchen, she was sorely tempted.

No wonder he'd accused her of taking over; just look at it! The counter was literally covered with baking ingredients—and over on the table, her failures. Two charred piecrusts and an enormous bowl of something that only a starving crow would eat.

If she'd had a grain of sense, she'd have tackled things one at a time instead of trying to do everything at once. Blame it on the fact that the few Thanksgivings she'd spent at home had been cold, uncomfortable affairs, with her father holed up in his greenhouse and her mother complaining that the turkey was underdone, the vegetables overdone and there was too much rum in the pie.

Unless Susan happened to be home. Then everything was magically transformed. Mother would shut up and listen for a change, and Dad would lean back in his chair with a fatuous grin on his face, listening to his favorite daughter tell about all the many ways she'd discovered to spend his money.

Susan liked nice things, and why shouldn't she? She'd been brought up to expect them as her due. She was also genuinely kind, and would never knowingly hurt a soul. Gale had often suspected that she only took those lavish vacations and bought herself all those outrageously expensive things to please their father.

On impulse, Gale hurried to her room the minute the kitchen was halfway presentable, and dug out her address book, returning with it to the study. It had been months since she'd heard from her sister, and suddenly, she needed to hear her voice, even if it did cost an arm and a leg.

Sax was on the phone. He glanced up as she barged through the door, the open address book in her hand. "Did you need something?"

Gale wilted like a morning glory yanked from the vine. "No. That is—nothing." She backed out. It had been a rotten idea, anyway. Why ruin Susan's holiday? Did they even celebrate Thanksgiving in Italy?

No, of course they didn't. At the moment, she didn't feel much like celebrating, either.

At a quarter to eleven the day before Thanksgiving, Enid drove up in a red Mercedes sports car. Her fiery red hair was tied back with a gold silk scarf, and she was wearing a hot pink sweater over snug scarlet pants.

"Hi, all," she called out gaily, waving an arm circled with six inches of silver bangles.

Gale had been sweeping the leaves off the front porch. Saxon had been replacing a hook on a shutter that had picked an inopportune moment to start banging. Neither of them had spoken half a dozen words all morning.

"Saxie, this is *mar*-velous!" the redhead called out as Sax edged through the boxwoods and went to meet her. "You didn't tell me how *big* this place was. It absolutely *drips* with atmosphere!" She threw her arms around Sax's neck, kicking one booted foot up behind her as she gave him an enthusiastic kiss.

Gale swatted a pile of oak leaves hard enough to send them sailing into the next county.

Chapter Nine

The evening turned out to be far more enjoyable than Gale had expected. She'd tried several excuses to keep from joining Sax and his guest at the barbecue place out on the highway, but they'd both insisted. Short of making an issue of it, there was little she could do.

That night she saw a different side of Sax. He was more open, more relaxed, and Gale put it down to Enid's influence. Who could remain grouchy in the presence of a cheerful, gregarious redhead who openly admitted that her sole mission in life was to marry a rich man and allow him to spoil her to his heart's content?

They took turns describing, in what Gale hoped were exaggerated terms, life on a windswept stretch of Oklahoma's panhandle that was so desolate that even the buzzards detoured around it.

"Basically, it's good land, though," Sax admitted. "Steppin' Creek's just suffering from too many years of neglect. The place was worn down to bedrock by the time Jay inherited it from his father. According to some of the older hands, John Jackson Mathis was a transplanted shoe salesman from Philadelphia who knew as much about ranching as I do about playing the French horn."

Enid giggled. "I don't know about your French horn, honey, but I've heard you singin' in the shower, and music is definitely not one of your talents! So what made a shoe salesman from Philly tackle ranchin'?" Elbows on the table, she was unself-consciously working on a slab of barbecued ribs.

"Expedience," Sax replied laconically. He was sitting beside Enid, across the table from Gale. "According to Tully, old J.J. went broke and headed west to make his fortune. Instead, he made the rancher's daughter. Papa produced a shotgun, and J.J. and his bride produced Jay Junior a few months later."

Red strands gleamed brightly against a black-clad shoulder as Enid leaned against Sax and giggled. Gale didn't know which was worse, to be here where she could watch them together, or to be somewhere else wondering what they were doing. She hadn't missed that remark about singing in the shower.

"Jay'll do all right," Sax said thoughtfully. "He joined the coast guard out of sheer frustration, but he's really hooked on the old place. Trouble was, his old man poured good money after bad trying to do something he had no feeling for. It didn't help that there was a long drought, and then an early freeze about the time Jay took over. He finally got fed up and took himself a breather, you might say."

Enid blotted her glossy lips on a paper napkin, removing the last tinge of Plum Pink lipstick. "So where do you come in? I thought the place belonged to you. The way they all call you Dude, I sort of thought they were kidding you about being top dog."

Shifting his long legs under the scarred table, Sax finished his beer and carefully replaced the bottle in the circle of its own moisture. Except for the glint of laughter in his eyes, he might have been deadly serious. "Why, darlin', the reason they call me Dude is because I thought the place was a dude ranch the first three years I was there. Plopped down a small fortune for the vacation of a lifetime before I finally began to suspect the truth."

Even Gale had to laugh. Not in her wildest imagination could she picture Saxon as a guest at a dude ranch. "I knew there had to be some good reason for those high-heeled boots of yours," she teased. "If they'd been a little fancier, I might have suspected you of being a country and western star."

"You heard the lady," Sax said, tipping his head toward Enid. "No talent. The truth is, Jay got in a bind one night in a poker game and tossed in the deed to the ranch. I happened to be holding a pretty good hand for a change, so I ended up with a half interest and a working arrangement. It suited us both."

"Oh, pooh!" Enid pouted. "I've been buttering up to the wrong man. Reckon Jay'd let me have a hand in remodeling that old barn of a ranch house?"

"It's J.J., honey," Sax teased, "not J.R."

The pangs of jealousy Gale had been suffering over since the redhead had showed up this morning had lightened considerably. If Enid, who was actually a part of Sax's other life, didn't know all there was to know about him, then perhaps the relationship wasn't quite as close as she'd imagined.

It was close enough, though. Too close for comfort.

Sax turned to the woman beside him. "How about trying some of the sliced pork, Enid? You can't get the real flavor of Eastern-style barbecue until you taste that."

"Spoken like a true rancher." Enid laughed and glanced down at her generous figure, well displayed in the hot pink sweater. "All you can think of is fattening up your stock."

"That's not *all* I think about," Sax responded gallantly.

By the time they got back home, Gale had come to several conclusions, one of which was that Enid was a thoroughly nice woman. With her wholesome, breezy sexuality, she'd be a perfect match for a man like Sax. He needed someone who could draw him out of those dark moods, someone who could make him forget the past and get on with the future.

Gale was obviously the wrong someone; she was a part of the past he needed to forget. There was no way he'd ever be able to look at her without being reminded of the woman who'd taken his mother's place in his father's affections, and in his own home. Or the adopted stepson with whom Richard had replaced his own flesh and blood.

But that wasn't the worst of it. He'd have to know what she'd done. She'd been aching to tell him, held back only by a lack of opportunity—and by a lack of courage.

Gale told herself that while he might eventually forgive her, he'd never quite bring himself to trust her.

In the back of his mind, like a dormant seed, would be the knowledge that she'd once stolen from him, taken things that had belonged in his family and sold them. In time, he'd forget that she'd had a perfectly valid reason and remember only her dishonesty.

That alone was enough to poison any chance they might have had for happiness.

The minute they got home that night, Gale excused herself on the pretext of work that needed doing. She'd planned to escape to the darkroom, but Sax caught up with her in the kitchen, catching her by the hand and swinging her around.

"Dammit, Gale, you don't have to do any cooking! I told you I'd made reservations for tomorrow."

"I wasn't planning to do any cooking," she said, snatching her hand away and holding it behind her. Evidently, he'd already used up his small store of geniality. "I hope you didn't include me in your plans for tomorrow."

"I damned well did!" Sax said dropping his hand. "Is there any reason why I shouldn't have?"

"If you'd bothered to consult me first, I could have told you that I have plans of my own," she said coolly.

Sax looked dumbfounded. "*What* plans?"

"I don't know that it's any of your business, but I do have friends, Saxon. I have my own interests, and now that Richard's better and you have someone to keep you company, I see no real need for me to stay on. I've been thinking about—"

"The hell you have!"

"You might let me finish a statement before you jump down my throat."

"I'll do more than jump down your throat," he threatened, and she took a step backward.

In spite of his menacing expression, Gale knew he wouldn't hurt her—not intentionally, at least. But if he thought she was going to hang around while he played footsie with another woman, he was sadly mistaken. She might be broke, but she wasn't stupid.

"You don't own me, Saxon," she said quietly. Making the most of her negligible height, Gale tilted her head back and dared him to contradict her.

His eyes went curiously flat. Before he could speak, Enid's voice called from the hall just outside the study.

"Saxie, I need help! I put another log on the fire, but it must have had a streak of lightwood in it. You'd better get in here."

With a muffled curse, Sax wheeled away, leaving Gale to stare after him. Damn the man! Damn him to perdition for making her fall in love with him when he had no intention of loving her back!

Thanksgiving morning dawned cold and drizzly, which suited Gale's mood to perfection. Her head was splitting, thanks to having stayed awake half the night waiting for the other two to go to bed.

She refused to wait for them to vacate the kitchen before she went in to cook her own breakfast. She had a lot to think about today, and she couldn't do her worries justice on an empty stomach.

"Hi, Gale, how many pancakes can you eat? I found some honey—you wouldn't happen to have any maple syrup, would you?"

Gale halted just inside the door and stared at the woman skillfully flipping pancakes onto a plate on the warming tray. "M-maple syrup?"

Enid shrugged, managing to look stunning in one of Mrs. McCrary's wraparound aprons over pink stretch pants and a matching sweater, worn with orange suede ankle boots. "Never mind. Me, I like 'em with marmalade, ice cream, preserves—anything sweet. Ever had 'em with whipped cream and Tia Maria? Scrumptious!"

"No, I don't think I ever did," Gale said weakly.

Enid pulled out a chair without pausing in what she was doing. "Take a load off, honey. I'll have your plate ready in a jiff. Saxie's down in the basement looking for a picnic basket. I didn't want to be a bother if you were expecting company here, so I talked him into showing me his Blue Ridge Mountains this afternoon. He said you had plans, but if you want to come along for the ride, I reckon we can squeeze you in."

Numbly, Gale accepted the stack of pancakes and stared at them. They were lighter and fluffier looking than anything she'd ever been able to produce. "No thanks, Enid. You two have fun."

"Your loss, my gain. Frankly, I'm looking forward to having him all to myself. I take it I'm not horning in on your personal territory?"

Gale shook her head, unable to trust her voice. The pancakes suddenly looked as if they might choke her, and she pushed her plate away untouched. "Don't be silly," she managed to say, practically tripping over her own feet as she rose again to pour herself a mug of coffee.

"Never can tell about these things." Enid flipped the last pancake onto the plate and switched off the burner, sliding the cast-iron griddle aside to cool. "Saxie!" she yelled in the general direction of the basement door, "Come an' get it!"

Still partially numbed by the way the big breezy woman had simply moved in and taken over, Gale reached for a pancake with her fingers and nibbled absently. "Yes, well...I guess Sax must have told you that I was—I mean, about my—"

"Your poor husband? Jay told me, honey. Sax's been keepin' in touch with the ranch by phone, but the old meanie never did get around to callin' me. I have to get all my news secondhand from Jay." Enid divided the stack onto two plates and began slathering butter over each layer. "If you want to know the truth, you're the main reason I'm here. Honey, I've got the hots for that man so bad I can't see straight. In all the time I've known him—well, it hasn't been all that long, I reckon—but once I set my sights on a man, I don't usually waste much time. Anyhow, this is the first time he's ever strayed farther than Amarillo, and I was scared witless he wasn't planning to come back. Then, when Jay told me there was this young widowed sister-in-law living in the same house with him..." She dumped half a jar of imported lime marmalade onto the stack, yelled for Sax once more and took an enormous bite.

"Well, you can see where I'd be worried," she reasoned when she could speak again. "I'm thirty-three years old—I bloomed early and enjoyed every minute of it, but I'm not going to be able to keep my looks forever. Now take a woman like yourself—you probably didn't even know the score until you were practically out of your teens. You'll still be a looker when you're an old lady—you've got that classy kind of bone structure."

Gale thought she must have murmured a few words of thanks, but she was so dazed by the frank appraisal she wasn't sure whether she'd even spoken aloud.

"Oh, my assets are solid enough at the moment," Enid said, somehow managing to chew and talk at the same time without giving offense. "But honey, I'm not kidding myself. Everything that bounces so nice now will be flopping in another few years."

She took another big bite, smiling as guilelessly as a puppy, and reached for the marmalade. "I worked as a waitress for five years just so I could go to college and catch me a rich husband. Trouble was, I was having so much fun I kept putting off making a decision until it was too late. By that time, seeing as I started later than the other kids, I was gettin' older, and the men were all gettin' younger. I said to myself, Enid, you dumb jerk, school's no place to find what you're looking for. So I got me a job where I'd be sure to meet a lot of rich, successful men."

Gale was enthralled, in spite of herself. "Yes—and then what?"

"Lawyers, honey. You gotta be rich to afford 'em. I got myself a job with the best lawyer in town. The best *single* lawyer, that is." She grinned, and again Gale made some sound that must have passed for a comment.

It was all the encouragement her chatty houseguest needed. Enid propped her elbows on the table and stared earnestly, if a bit nearsightedly, at her hostess. "I mean, who uses lawyers? Rich folks, right? And if all else failed, I could always marry my boss, right? But then one day a few months ago I was aimin' for the only parking place left in front of the post office, when who should I hook bumpers with but this prime cut of Evanshaw beef, with a big ranch thrown in as a bonus." She lifted her dark eyebrows expressively. "Honey, by the time we got around to swapping insurance agents' names, I was pantin' so hard my tongue got sunburned!"

Gale, breakfast forgotten, stared in open fascination. She'd never met anyone even faintly like Enid Brachman. She didn't know whether to applaud her panache or kick her out on her shapely butt.

At the sound of Sax's boots on the narrow wooden stairs that led to the basement, both women turned toward the door. "Your breakfast's gettin' cold, honey," Enid declared cheerfully. "Come on now, I've got it all buttered up and sweetened just the way you like it."

"Gale, is that your darkroom?" Sax crossed to the sink, looking taller than ever. The faded navy flannel shirt stretched across his broad chest, closely matching in color the service-issue jeans that hugged his narrow hips and long, muscular thighs like a well-worn glove.

"What? Oh—that. Yes, it's mine. At least the equipment's mine. Your father gave me permission to use the room." Her eyes held a look that Enid would have recognized easily if all her attention hadn't been focused on Saxon.

"What about those barrels in the other room?"

Gale waited until Sax had seated himself at the table. Enid brought his plate from the warming tray and poured his coffee, leaning over him so that the back of his head was nestled between her generous breasts.

Gale quickly turned away to stare out through the window. The gray drizzle continued to channel its way down the tall panes, hiding the distant mountain ridges and giving the surrounding countryside the look of an impressionist painting. "What about them?"

"What's in them? What're they doing there? And what the devil would you need a darkroom for?" Ignoring the stack of pancakes, glistening with butter and swimming in sourwood honey, Sax reached for his coffee.

With as much dignity as she could muster, Gale said, "I use the darkroom for my work."

"Your work? What work?"

Sooner or later she'd have told him, but this was hardly the time she'd have chosen. Not with that skeptical look on his face and Enid avidly lapping up every word. "I dabble in photography," she said stiffly.

"And the barrels? Do you use those in your work, too?"

Oh, Lord, what timing! "Look, Sax, do we have to go into this right now? It's Thanksgiving Day! You've got plans, I've got plans, and I'm sure Enid doesn't want to hear an inventory of the contents of your father's basement."

"Don't mind me, honey, I'm game for anything," the redhead chirped.

Sax shot her a sour look and swore under his breath, and Enid grinned at Gale. "Sweet, isn't he? Snarls worse'n a treed possum when he's hungry," she observed cheerfully, as if Sax weren't even present. "If he wasn't rich and so damned good-looking, he'd hardly be worth the trouble, but I've already put in a good four months on him, and I hate like the dickens to waste time."

* * *

Gale got off first. She was reasonably certain that

Sax didn't plan on visiting Richard until later in the day; perhaps not at all, now that he had his hands full of his hot-pink redhead. She planned her strategy accordingly, driving directly out to Laurel Hill, where she visited until just after one.

To her delight, Richard opened his eyes for a few minutes before letting his lids drift down again. It happened several times as she played one of his tapes and talked about the latest political crisis. Gale described the clearing that was taking place west of town for a new shopping mall, and then tried to think of something cheerful and seasonal to say to a man who probably wouldn't be enjoying a holiday at home any time in the near future.

"Less than a month until Christmas. Do you mind if I prune the balsam fir to make a wreath? It smells so wonderful, don't you think so? Cedar and balsam and oranges always smell like Christmas to me."

As she stood beside his bed, her hand on his as she said goodbye, Gale wondered how it was that this man had come to mean so much to her in such a short time. Even when he'd been well, he'd had very little to say to her, except for that one occasion when she'd happened to catch him in a nostalgic mood.

Empathy. It was probably just a perfectly normal response of a healthy person to someone in Richard's condition, she rationalized. It was only natural to feel sympathetic, and she was inclined to be even more so because of the way Olivia had acted. The fact that he was Saxon's father could have been something to do with it, too.

The Evanshaw arrogance was gone now, and those blue eyes he shared with his son had lost most of their luster, but there was so much of Saxon in him, nevertheless. Perhaps that was the reason Gale felt a bond she couldn't begin to understand. Any more than she understood her feelings for Sax. They were simply there.

"Richard, I need you," she said softly. "Please get well and come home again. Sax needs you, too."

It was then that his fingers moved. She couldn't have been mistaken about it. Those wasted fingers had jumped—a little more than a twitch, actually—and she'd been too elated to remember what she might have said to bring about the reaction.

Afterward, she tried to reconstruct it. She couldn't recall saying anything unusual that would have triggered a response. She could only conclude that it had been accidental. Both Sax and the nurse had reported small movements before, but this was the first sign Gale herself had seen that recovery—even partial recovery—might not be so impossible, after all.

It was late by the time she got away from Laurel Hill, and she was starved. None of them had done justice to Enid's pancakes. Dinner at the Copper Kettle with the regulars whose families lived too far away to visit didn't sound half-bad. The way her luck in the kitchen had been running lately, she'd have ruined a perfectly good turkey.

The cashier gave her a friendly greeting, and before she'd even removed her coat, Gale had been invited to join several tables. Smiling her thanks to the others, she slid into a booth with the woman whose greenhouse of potted palms she'd photographed for the jungle scene in her book, and one of her friends.

"I've been craving a big slice of pecan pie all week," Gale confided.

"Dream on, honey," said the waitress who'd come to take their order. "Cookie ran out of vanilla extract last night and dumped a shot glass of brandy into every single pie. You wouldn't believe the run we've had on them things this morning. Turkey and the works?"

"Turkey and the works," Gale agreed, with only a fleeting thought to the pair who were probably dining on Hunting Ridge's famous smoked wild turkey about now.

It was late afternoon by the time Gale turned off the state road onto the Evanshaw driveway. The rain had ended, giving way to a pale, colorless sunset. It looked dreary. She *felt* dreary. And she hated the feeling.

At least after the meal she'd put away today, she wouldn't need to eat again for a week. With Enid to see to Saxon's needs, this would be a perfect time to get caught up on all her darkroom work.

At the thought of Saxon and his redhead parked somewhere on one of the overlooks along the parkway, fogged in by steamy windows as they ignored the spectacular Blue Ridge scenery, her mood deteriorated further. If all they'd wanted was privacy, they should have booked a room at Sugar Ridge Inn.

"Cheerful thought," she grumbled, letting herself in through the utility room. She'd somehow managed to keep her mind occupied for most of the day without once touching on the subject of Sax and his relationship with Enid Brachman. With any luck, she could avoid thinking about them for the next few years. Or until it stopped hurting, whichever came first.

Work was what she needed. If she could just put her mind on hold long enough to get absorbed in what she was doing, she'd be just fine. The book was nearly finished, the bills had slowed up for the past few days and Richard was showing definite signs of improvement. That was enough to rejoice over.

She mixed up fresh solutions and stacked the contact sheets already printed on the table by the door so she wouldn't forget to take them upstairs with her. She'd process these last few rolls, print some more contact sheets and then take everything up to the study where she had a decent light to work by. By the time she went to bed tonight, she'd have selected the negatives she wanted to enlarge. Tomorrow, she'd shoot the last few scenes, and tomorrow night she'd develop, print and get set up to start on the rough enlargements to see how much retouching would be needed.

Working automatically, she ran the film through the several necessary steps, her mind busy with plans for the future. Feeling almost euphoric, she told herself that with careful scheduling and a bit of luck, she could have the whole works ready to express to New York in a week's time.

After that, she'd give this house one last thorough turnout and start looking for a place of her own. Surely Tad Benton would have returned by then. Or Olivia would have been in touch. They owed her almost four hundred dollars, money she'd drawn from her own account to pay the household and nursing home bills.

As for the pieces she'd had to sell, that was a different thing altogether. Some of them might still be in Mr. Crump's hands, but most of them would be long gone. Her only consolation lay in the fact that Olivia had packed away almost everything that had belonged to the first Mrs. Evanshaw, indicating that she hadn't cared much for them.

As for Sax's views on the matter, Gale didn't even want to think about it.

It was just after nine when she went upstairs. She'd changed into her working clothes, which consisted of corduroys and sweatshirt so stained with chemicals that a few more stains wouldn't matter. Her thick-soled walking shoes were a must on the concrete floors.

Carrying her magnifying glass and the stack of proof sheets, contact prints of every negative on each roll she'd taken, she headed for the study to leave them there while she took a quick shower and made herself a pot of fresh coffee. Then, warm, clean and comfortable, she'd begin selecting which shots to blow up and which to retouch.

The fragrant smell of burning applewood met her at the door. Saxon unfolded himself from the couch, a newspaper dangling from his fingers. "I was beginning to wonder if you'd taken up permanent residence down there," he said quietly.

The huskiness that was so characteristic of his deep voice raised goose bumps on her arms. "I didn't know you were back."

"It wasn't a good day for sight-seeing, after all."

"Too misty," Gale murmured, her eyes trapped in the sapphire depths of his.

"Too misty," he repeated. "How about you? Did you have a good day?"

She nodded. Later on, she'd tell him about Richard's fingers twitching under hers. But not now. Now she was far too conscious of the way his gaze moved over her. She knew she looked like a scarecrow. She probably smelled even worse. All she wanted was to get away without making a complete fool of herself. "I need to get washed up."

"You're probably cold. The furnace never did heat the basement very well. Come stand by the fire."

Come into my parlor, said the spider to the fly. "Not on your life!" she retorted.

Sax lifted his dark brows in surprise, and Gale realized what she'd said. "I mean—I only meant—look, let me go get a quick shower and change into something a little more respectable. Where's Enid?"

"Sacked out."

It was Gale's turn to look surprised. "Already?"

"We ran into Billy Trent and his girlfriend at the club, and drove out to Billy's place afterwards to sample some locally produced wine. Enid's an enthusiastic sampler."

Gale's lips tilted in amusement. Enid was enthusiastic about everything she tackled, and if she drank with the same appetite she brought to the breakfast table, she probably wouldn't be able to lift her head off the pillow tomorrow.

"I like her a lot, Sax. She's rather—unexpected, but she seems to be thoroughly nice."

"Enid's all right," Sax said curtly.

Gale would have given everything she owned—which wasn't all that impressive a statement at the moment—to know just how he felt about the flamboyant redhead. She hurried away to shower and change, leaving him to stare at the fire, the paper forgotten at his side.

Sax needed to do some serious thinking about the two women in his life, although the outcome was already a foregone conclusion. For a little while, Enid

had been a bright spot in an otherwise grueling life.
Sax had never labored under any delusions as to why
she'd welcomed him into her life and into her bed.
Having been born into a dirt-poor family near the
Kansas border, she'd worked and schemed for the sort
of future she wanted, making no bones about the fact
that security came first, fun a close second.

The woman who'd been born with nothing and
fought her way up was perfectly open about her deep-
seated need for security. The one who'd been born
with everything and then lost it all had reacted in an
entirely different way.

Eleven years ago Sax had learned a hard lesson
about judging someone you loved. It had cost him a
father. Was he prepared to take that risk again? Would
Gale believe him if he told her that it no longer mattered to him what she'd done?

Sax raked his fingers through his hair, leaving the
thick layers even more disheveled than usual. No
amount of rationalizing could make right out of
wrong. Yet, all that seemed irrelevant now.

If he'd stayed in Oklahoma and never come east
again, he might have married Enid and been reasonably content with his lot. Neither of them was looking for more than the other could offer, which might
be a sounder basis for marriage than most.

At least, he'd thought so until recently. Until he'd
looked into a pair of smoky-topaz eyes and seen his
whole life flash past.

She could have been a convicted felon and he still
wouldn't be able to keep from loving her. All he knew
was that something inside of him reached out to
something inside of her. It was the same way with
these old hills, these ancient, familiar Blue Ridge

Mountains. They claimed a part of him that could never belong to the arid west.

He'd walked into two traps when he'd walked through the door of Saxon Hall. Now he was going to have to make arrangements to turn over his share of Steppin' Creek to Jay. Sax hoped he hadn't hurt Enid's pride too terribly when he'd tried to explain that there was no future for them together.

He wanted Gale. He also wanted his home and his father. One way or another, he was going to have the woman, and if he was lucky, he'd have the rest as well.

Chapter Ten

After frantically pulling out and discarding every garment she owned, Gale finally selected a flowing, cowl-necked hostess gown of honey-colored velvet that had been a gift from Susan. Gale could easily picture her sister lounging around the palazzo on her quiet evenings at home in something this glamorous and impractical. Her own lounge wear ran more to sweatshirts and bunny slippers.

The time had come to clear her conscience by telling Sax exactly what she'd done and why she'd had to do it. She couldn't carry this awkward burden alone another day. It would be embarrassing, but knowing she looked her best might make it easier to say what had to be said. Or at least to say enough so that he'd understand the rest without her having to wade through all the agonizing details.

"Sax, we need to talk," she announced from the door of the study a few minutes later.

Saxon felt something inside him melt and begin to give way, like a frozen creek at the first thaw. "All right, little dove, we'll talk then." He'd much rather pull her down beside him and make love to her until the rest of the world disappeared, but if she wanted to talk, then talk they would.

With his eyes following her every step, Gale moved to one of the two leather wing chairs and seated herself. Crossing one leg over the other, she carefully arranged her flowing robe, to hide the tip of her slippered foot. At the last minute, she'd put aside the jeweled satin mules that matched the velvet hostess gown in favor of something slightly more comfortable. Not to mention safer. Now, she lifted her chin and steeled herself to do what must be done.

Sax was in no hurry. Waiting for her to compose herself and come to the point allowed him time to appreciate the beauty that was so uniquely hers. Tonight, with her hair swept up and that long, flowing gown on, she looked as regal as any princess.

That is, she did until one encountered the tip of a yellow bunny slipper nervously twitching the soft hemline.

"Well," she said finally, after clearing her throat once or twice. "As you mentioned once before—I mean, you've obviously noticed that—" Gale cleared her throat again. She'd known it was going to be difficult, but she hadn't expected it to be impossible. If he'd only stop *looking* at her that way, she might get her tongue working again.

"Saxon, I want you to know—that is, you already know, but I wanted to explain— Well, actually, I've—

ah—taken a few small items that I had no right to take." The last few words came out in a breathless rush.

A few small items? Sax figured it might come to roughly a hundred grand without even knowing the details. The rugs and paintings alone were probably worth that much. He could feel a muscle in his jaw begin to twitch.

"You have to understand my situation," Gale went on earnestly, while Sax loosened an already unbuttoned collar as if it were strangling him. There had to be some way to frame her confession so that it wouldn't sound quite so... incriminating.

On the other hand, what good was a confession that didn't incriminate? Closing her eyes to the consequences, she barged ahead. "Saxon, I simply didn't know what else to do. I'd hoped my jewelry would be enough, but it wasn't, so I picked a few things I didn't think anyone would miss and sold them. For cash. To Mr. Crump. He's local, but he's discreet." She swallowed, unable to bring herself to meet his eyes. "Of course, I probably only got a fraction of what the things were worth, but beggars can't be choosers. I tried to hold out, Sax, I really did, but things just kept piling up. I guess I just... panicked."

She waited a hundred years for him to say something. Finally, he spoke. "I see."

"Do you?" She exclaimed eagerly. "Sax, it was only because the bank got things all messed up— computer error, probably, although from the way Mr. Bahanian looked at me, you'd think I'd walked into his blasted bank with a gun and a ski mask. He wouldn't let me use the household account, and I had no way of knowing when either Olivia or Tad Benton would get back. The bills started coming and I just couldn't afford to wait.''

Feeling immensely better already, she searched his face for some clue as to what he was thinking. ''Can you understand how desperate I felt? Everyone was gone, and suddenly everybody was wanting money, and I was all alone here, and... I really haven't been here all that long. Not long enough to feel as if I belonged here. So I just went ahead and—did it.''

''You did *what*, Gale?'' Sax asked softly, and she stared at him, puzzled. ''Go ahead—say it. Say the actual word.''

''Haven't you been listening?'' she wailed.

''You said you—what was your phrase, you *picked* a few things? You *sold* a few items? You went ahead and *did it*?'' His voice hardened. ''What is it you're trying to tell me Gale? How can you expect me to help you if you can't even bring yourself to use the word?''

She didn't flinch. He wanted his pound of flesh? He'd have it. She owed him that much, at least. Her eyes might have glistened a bit more brightly for a moment, and her chin definitely had a wobble to it, but Gale looked him directly in the eyes and spelled it out for him. ''I *stole* from you. Is that what you wanted to hear? I hope you feel better now, because I certainly don't!'' She paused only long enough to take another deep, shuddering breath. ''I thought I would, but I don't,'' she whispered.

And then she was on her feet, dodging the ottoman, skirting the coffee table, racing for the door, with Sax two steps behind her.

''Gale!''

''Leave me alone,'' she cried brokenly as he grabbed at a long, flowing sleeve.

"Dammit, come back here! I'm not through with you yet!"

She spun around at that, only to find herself trapped in his arms. Unable to see him clearly through the tears that filmed her eyes, she glared at the dark triangular thatch that showed in the vee of his shirt. "Go ahead and prosecute me then, but I'm warning you, if you throw me in jail, I won't ever be able to pay you back! As it is, I might be able to reimburse you within a few months for—for most of what I took. *Stole.*" She made herself repeat the hated word, rubbing salt into an already burning wound.

He tightened his arms around her, and rocked her gently, crooning words she didn't want to hear. Her own tears were choking her—the last thing she wanted was his pity!

"If you're thinking of trying to—to rehabilitate me, then you can just—stuff it!" she whispered furiously. "I'm *not* a thief! I'm *not*, no matter what you think!"

"Gale, please," Sax said gently, his voice a comforting rumble just above her ear. "I think I understand what happened, and why. But it's important that you understand, too. That's the only reason I pushed you, sweetheart. I want us to start with everything out in the open. No shadows between us. No secrets. I grew up in a house full of secrets, and I was too dumb to know what was going on. It damn near killed me when I found out the truth."

In spite of her shame, her anger and embarrassment, Gale was unable to resist the sweet coercion of Saxon's arms, the rough caress of his words. "If it means anything to you, Sax, I've hated every minute of it—sneaking into Mr. Crump's shop, hoping no one I knew would see me. I felt so miserable."

"You'll never have to feel that way again, I promise you, darling." He pressed a kiss on the blue vein that shadowed her temple, then moved his lips over her cheek. It felt cool and softer than the velvet in his arms. "I'll always take care of you. You'll never have to feel that desperate again."

Gale grew very still as his words penetrated the yoke of guilt she couldn't quite manage to discard. Surely he wasn't implying that he...cared for her? Cared quite a lot, in fact? With her pride in shreds, she was in no shape to play guessing games.

"Sax, what are you trying to tell me? You said no more secrets, exactly what do you mean when you say you'll take care of me?"

"If my words didn't get the message across, then maybe I'd better try something a little more graphic." Leaning against the door frame, he drew her tightly against him, spreading his legs so that she stood wedged in the fork of his thighs. Tilting her face, he captured her lips and parted them easily.

By the time he lifted his head again, they were both trembling. Sax dropped his hands to her hips, holding her against his throbbing body. "Graphic enough for you?"

Gale's laughter was soft and breathless as she gazed up at him. "Saxon, is it me, or is there just something about having a confessed criminal in your arms that turns you on?"

If his own laughter sounded a trifle forced, Gale was too euphoric to notice. "Good thing I didn't go into law enforcement, isn't it?" he asked.

"If I'd known a little polite larceny was all it took to get your attention, I'd have probably turned to a life of crime when I was thirteen. I had a dreadful crush on you then, did you know that?''

He brought her back against his chest as he stared thoughtfully at the stairway across the foyer. ''Thirteen, hmm? You might have managed to steal my heart, honey, but I doubt that you'd have won my body.''

With the sweet thunder of his heart under her cheek, Gale grinned. ''Never underestimate the resourcefulness of a determined woman, Evanshaw. If I'd hidden my glasses, unbraided my hair and jammed a long-stemmed rose in my braces, you'd never have known what hit you.''

He gave a shout of laughter and swept her up in his arms, then turned back into the study and sank down onto the couch, settling her comfortably on his lap.

Gale snuggled closer, burying her face in his throat to inhale the heady scent of his body. ''Of course, you might have had to overlook a few minor flaws, including crossed eyes and a figure like a tree frog.''

''Oh, I don't know—I'd probably have seen the potential, even then. The crossed eyes did clear up eventually, after all, and there's still hope for the figure.''

While he explored a few unfroglike curves, Gale relaxed and let herself be warmed by the miracle that Sax loved her enough to understand why she'd had to do what she did.

Toying with the buttons of his shirt, she tackled the one remaining problem that stood between them. ''Sax, what about Enid?''

''What about her?''

But he knew what she meant. Settling her more firmly on his lap, Sax searched for a way to make Gale understand that even though he was fond of Enid, she had never even come close to touching that secret place inside him that had been waiting through the ages for Gale Chandler to grow up.

"Enid and I—" He sought a polite way of describing a rather basic relationship. "We enjoyed each other's company for a while. She's a good companion. Actually, I admire her in a lot of ways." He could feel the sigh that moved through her whole body, and he had to restrain himself forcefully from crushing her in his arms. "I admire Beverly Sills and Mother Teresa, too, honey, but that doesn't mean I want to marry them."

All the strength seemed to flow right out of her legs through the soles of her feet as she caught the implication. Dare she believe him? Was there a tactful way of asking a man his intentions? "Does Enid know how you feel?"

"She does now. I think she sort of put two and two together the first time she saw us together, but in case she didn't, I pretty well spelled it out to her on the way to the club today."

"Poor Enid. No wonder she sampled your friend's wines so enthusiastically."

"Poor Enid will land on her feet, sweetheart. The cousin she's headed up to Richmond to see tomorrow is male, single, an investment banker and of the shirt-tail variety."

"You mean a third or a fourth cousin?"

Sax nodded, his hands busily engaged in searching out the velvet beneath the velvet. "He won't know what hit him. Can you imagine Enid bursting into the life of a staid investment banker?"

"Boggles the mind." She grinned. "I wonder who'll register the collision first, seismologists or astronomers." And then, before she could lose her nerve, she whispered, "Sax, do you—when you were talking about Beverly Sills and Mother Teresa, did you mean that you might want to marry *me*?"

"Isn't that what I said?"

"Not exactly," Gale replied dryly.

"It's what I meant."

"So that you can make an honest woman of me?"

There was a high flush on his angular cheekbones, and an unmistakable hardness pressing against her hip. "My reasons at the moment are pretty obvious, and honesty doesn't have a whole lot to do with them."

Gale felt a melting heat begin to flow through her body when he stroked his fingertips over the curve of her thigh. Whatever his reasons, she wanted him more than she'd ever wanted anything in her whole life. She only wished she could think a bit more objectively now that the moment had come.

"Remind me," she whispered breathlessly, "never to sit on your lap when I have anything serious to discuss with you."

"We'll sit across the table from each other, I promise." He inched his hand farther, toying with the lace of her panties.

"How about a teleconference?" she countered. "Long distance." She lay back in his arms, offering him the freedom of her body. A heavy, primitive need began hammering out a message low in her body that quickly spread. When she felt the backs of his fingers begin a slow, rhythmic stroking of the narrow, guarded path between her thighs, she whimpered softly.

"I think we'd better go to your room while I can still walk," Sax said gruffly.

"We don't have to go," Gale murmured.

"Honey, the study's not the most private room in the house, and I'm not sure I've got the strength to get us both up the stairs tonight."

Besides which, Enid was on the second floor. Sax didn't mention that; he didn't have to. Sliding off his lap, she took his hand and drew him to his feet, but instead of moving, Sax brought her gently against his aroused body, groaning softly as he tortured them both.

"It's been so long," he said.

"More than a week," Gale replied quickly. Hadn't she counted each day, each night, even while they were playing musical beds at a motel in Asheville while Richard was in the hospital?

"I missed you—Gale, you'll never know how much I wanted the right to crawl into your bed and hold on to you, darling."

"You always had that right, Sax. Didn't you know?"

Instead of replying, he lifted her in his arms and carried her swiftly through the shadowy foyer, into the west wing, pausing before her bedroom door. "Is this it?"

Wordlessly, Gale nodded. It wasn't as large as his room, nor as well appointed. Nor as warm, she remembered tardily. She'd shut off her register in the hope of postponing the day when the oil ran out and she'd have to explain to Sax about the whole mess.

Now it no longer mattered. He'd seen the bills; she'd confessed; he understood everything.

Neither of them noticed the temperature, though. Between them, they generated enough heat to warm a room twice as large, a bed twice as big.

"My beautiful dove," Sax whispered after he'd slipped the long velvet gown over her head.

"Don't you mean your little frog?"

But for the first time in her life, Gale felt truly beautiful. Under the spell of Sax's magic hands and the warm glow of his eyes, she felt desirable and desired, worthy of being loved.

Pausing only long enough to shed his own clothes, Sax followed her down onto the bed. She reached out to him, hungry for the feel of his hard shoulders, the wild silk that covered his chest and trailed down the flat slab of his stomach, to swirl around his navel before it broadened into a dark nest for his aggressive masculinity.

He traced the curving outline of her lips with his tongue, teased the corners and then darted hungrily between them. Carefully, he supported most of his weight on his arms, but she wanted to feel it, wanted to cradle him between her thighs, wanted to take him into her body. Once more she was impatient to experience all of him, to know again the shattering ecstasy that lay waiting for them just over the horizon.

Tugging at his shoulders, she drew him down so that her breasts were flattened against his chest. Soft against hard, hard against soft, she savored the many differences between their two bodies. She trailed her hands over his back, twisting under him in order to reach his lean hips, digging her nails into the resilient flesh. "Please, I want to make you feel good—tell me how."

Sax groaned and rolled partly onto his side, covering one small breast so that the sensitive tip nudged insistently at his palm. "Ah, sweet heaven, if you made me feel any better, I'd explode."

She lowered her head and found one of his nipples half hidden in the dense swirls of hair. Sweeping it with her tongue, she then nipped it gently between her teeth. Encouraged by his leaping response, she lavished still more attention on him.

Finally, Sax lifted her away. "Wait, sweetheart," he gasped. "Give me a minute first, will you?"

She'd have given him her life if he'd asked for it. Impatiently, she waited while he turned away and fumbled in the darkened room for his pants. After a moment, he turned back to her.

"I didn't protect you the last time, and I wasn't sure if you were doing anything."

Wordlessly, she shook her head. "It's been so long—more than two years. I should have thought about it."

Two years? Sax frowned. She'd only been widowed a year. One of these days he'd find out more about her marriage. On the other hand, it was a part of a past that could only hurt them both. It was time to move beyond all that, into the future.

"Maybe someday, if you're willing, we might . . ." He let it go unfinished, but Gale sensed his meaning as clearly as if he'd spoken the words aloud. The thought of carrying their child was so sweet it brought tears to her eyes.

"Your father will like that, darling," she whispered. "So will I."

He loved her then, with great care and great skill, bringing them both to a plateau of pleasure even more splendid than before. During the long hours of the night, Sax taught her more about herself than she'd learned in all her nearly twenty-six years. In return, Gale set loose the bonds of her imagination, loving freely and without restraint, until he surged into her one final time, and they slept in each others' arms.

It was late when Gale awoke. She knew before she ever opened her eyes that Saxon was no longer beside her. A dozen small aches in various parts of her body attested to the vigorous exercise of the night before. His scent was still faint on her pillow, hinting of citrus and spice, but the warmth was gone.

Flopping over onto her back, she squinted one eye open and then laughed aloud. Someone—it had to be Saxon—had carefully lined up her whole shabby menagerie across the foot of the bed. Boy, with his shaggy yarn hair and patched overalls. Golly, with his rumpled, scarred coat. Tripod, the three-legged elephant, and even Griselda, the fat striped cat with the litter of kittens stored in a zipped pouch in her belly.

She had to laugh, picturing Saxon's face when he'd wakened to see that motley crew staring at him from every available surface. It was hard to imagine that Sax didn't know all there was to know about her. But then, she'd never told him about her book, for the simple reason that everyone else she'd ever told had ridiculed her ambitions. Everyone except Susan, but Susan wasn't here.

Richard hadn't laughed, but that was probably because he'd been buried in the *Wall Street Journal* when the topic had first come up. After that she'd avoided discussing it whenever possible.

If Saxon laughed at her project, she'd die. In spite of the lack of encouragement, Gale still believed in herself and her ability. It meant something to know that she'd managed to interest an editor with a proposal and a few sample photos, but it would kill her if Sax dismissed her work as amateurish posturing.

"So instead, we let him think I'm some kind of kook who collects battered toys, huh, gang? Not that you're not a great-looking bunch, you understand, but it takes a real connoisseur to appreciate a dog who sports more Band-Aids than he does fleas, and a cat who looks as if she's about to give birth to a giant armadillo."

Her eagerness, as well as the smell of freshly brewed coffee, served to lure her out of bed. Taking time only to step under the shower, brush her hair and throw on her robe, Gale hurried out to see if she'd dreamed the whole unbelievably wonderful night. One look at Sax's face and she'd know.

But it was Enid's face that told the story.

"To the victor go the spoils—isn't that what they used to say in those old gladiator movies?" Enid poked dispiritedly at a slice of bacon on her plate.

Gale toned down her smile, feeling that the radiance she felt might not be entirely diplomatic under the circumstances. "Good morning, Enid. The coffee smells wonderful. Is there any left?"

"Sure, help yourself. I made a potful. Sax and I both had a cup before he left, but there's plenty more."

"He's gone?" Unable to hide her disappointment, Gale dropped down onto a chair.

"Said something about a couple of errands. Don't worry, honey, he'll be back. You've got him hog-tied, fair and square."

Enid left within the hour. "I won't wait around. I called Willis this morning, and he's expecting me."

"Willis?" Gale was helping carry out the matching fuchsia luggage.

"Aunt Lulu's husband's sister's son. I think. Anyway, he's a hustler, same as I am. If he looks like a good prospect, we might team up." She beamed a smile that had dimples dancing in her cheeks, although it didn't quite hide the shadows around her eyes. "Between the two of us, we could own Virginia and half of east Texas within five years."

Gale was going over contact proofs with a magnifying glass when Saxon got back. She slid the stack of photos under the *Daily Observer* and went to meet him.

"Enid said you had some errands. She left about forty-five minutes ago." Hold me, kiss me, tell me that I didn't dream it all, she pleaded silently.

His smile wasn't quite as spontaneous as hers, but as if he'd read her mind, Sax tossed his leather jacket across a chair and held out his arms. She flew to him, and he caught her up and lifted her off the floor, burying his face in her throat. "Morning, sweetness. Didn't you get my message?"

"Did you leave one?" Sliding down his lean body in the circle of his arms, Gale made no attempt to hide her feelings. Happiness spilled over her like sunshine on a hot August day.

"I told those bozos to keep you in bed until I got back, but I should have known they couldn't be trusted. A shiftier-looking bunch I've yet to see."

Gale tried to look indignant but failed. "Watch it, Evanshaw. You're talking about my best friends. They might look a little seedy at the moment, but they're going to be rich and famous any day now."

"I'll take your word for it. I'm learning that it never pays to go by appearances."

Her face hidden against the solid wall of a flannel-clad chest, Gale's smile wavered. "Let's not talk about that anymore," she said. "I'm still embarrassed, no matter how decent you've been about it. Sax, you have to understand—"

Burrowing a fist under her chin, he lifted her face and smiled down at her. "I do understand, darling. I said so, didn't I? And you were the one who said let's not talk about it, so what do you suggest we do instead?"

Her smile flickered on again. "There's a guest room to be stripped. And the laundry. Mrs. McCrary won't be here until Monday."

"Not exactly what I had in mind," he teased, tracing the contour of her cheek and then exploring with a fingertip the small, flat shell of her ear.

"Mmm . . . The floor's open for suggestions."

"The floor's a bit cold and hard for what I had in mind." He kissed first one eyelid and then the other, and Gale purred in sheer contentment.

"So much for housework," she said with a shuddering little gasp as he took the lobe of one ear between his teeth. "Go ahead—lead me astray."

Sax laughed at that. Reluctantly, he put her away from him. "I'm not sure who's doing the leading and who's doing the following, but at the moment, maybe we'd better settle for talking after all. Which do you want first, the good news or the bad?" Taking her hand, he led her back into the study and started to draw her down onto his lap.

"Hold it—this sounds like serious business. I'd better sit over here, or I'll never get any news at all. You know what happens when I sit on your lap."

Sax chuckled. "Spontaneous combustion, you mean? Remind me to check out the sprinkler system." Then he sobered. "Gale, I took the liberty of depositing funds in your bank account. I thought that as long as we're going to be married anyway..."

It took a minute, but when the words registered, she stiffened. "You *what*?"

"I said—well, first, let me tell you what's been going on with Benton. That's the bad news."

"Wait a minute, back up. Now what was that about your giving me money? Is that your idea of good news?" she demanded incredulously. "Saxon, I won't have it. I absolutely refuse to allow you to give me anything, after—well, you know what I mean," she muttered, unable to meet his eyes. Her fingers twisted frantically in her lap as she tried to think of some way of making him understand that her pride had already suffered a crippling blow. How could she accept his charity until she'd had a chance to make up to him for what she'd done?

"Dammit, look at me, Gale! Do you think I like having to go into all this? There's nothing I'd like more than dumping the whole damned business and taking you away from here. Unfortunately, I can't do that. With Dad in the shape he's in, someone has to assume responsibility around here."

"Protect the Evanshaws' interests, you mean," she said bitterly. She'd been a Chandler a lot longer than she'd been an Evanshaw, but if the truth were known, she'd never felt as if she really belonged to either family. And never had she felt more alone than she did at that moment.

"Yes, I do mean that. But before you start heaping guilt onto your plate, you may as well know that I've been making a few quiet inquiries lately."

"At the bank, you mean?"

"There, too. Luther Bahanian told me about the—um, mistake you made."

"The mistake *I* made! You mean the mistake *he* made!"

Patiently, Sax tried to formulate the words in such a way as not to hurt her any more than she'd already been hurt. It killed him to have to do this at all, but it was too much to be swept under the rug and forgotten. "He said you wrote several checks on an account you weren't authorized to use, and that even if you had been, there'd have been insufficient funds to cover them all."

Without a vestige of color in her face, Gale lifted her eyes to the brilliant intensity of his. "I don't care what Mr. Bahanian told you, I *was* authorized to use that account. By Olivia. Before she left, she brought home one of those signature cards the bank has, and I signed it."

"And turned it in to the bank?"

"Olivia did that." Gale frowned. "At least she said she was going to do it when she picked up her traveler's checks. You don't suppose she could have forgotten it?"

"It still wouldn't explain why she'd offer to give you access to a worthless account. There was barely enough in there to pay the service charge."

Gale's temper reached flash point. "Oh, so now you're telling me I somehow managed to raid an account I supposedly wasn't even able to use? Come on, Saxon, make up your mind what you're accusing me of!"

Sax shook his head. It was beginning to throb quite badly, but he needed to get through this business and put it behind him—behind both of them. "Unless Benton had something to do with that, too," he murmured.

"Why don't you cable the ship and ask Olivia what's going on? Maybe she's in on this great robbery scheme of yours, too. Maybe she's not even aboard the cruise ship," she said a little shrilly. "She's probably in Monte Carlo right this minute, gambling away thousands and thousands of dollars!"

"She's on board the *Princess*, all right. I've already checked that out. She boarded in Miami and hasn't missed a meal since."

"Well, at least she'll be in good shape to straighten this mess out when she gets home," Gale said angrily. "She could hardly eat a bite before she left."

"She'll need her strength if what I'm beginning to suspect is true."

"And what you suspect is that I've been—"

"Not you, Gale—Benton! At least, not you alone. And honey, if it helps any, not for one moment did I believe that you had any idea what was going on with the bulk of Dad's finances. What you did was nothing compared to what Benton's done."

Somewhere deep inside her, Gale felt all her shiny new dreams begin to wither and crumble into dust. She should have known it would never work. Sax might claim to have forgiven her, but he'd never be able to forget.

"You're saying that Mr. Benton has been dishonest?" she repeated woodenly.

"I'm saying that it's beginning to look like Benton has systematically shifted every liquid asset out of Dad's estate and into a series of different accounts in foreign banks that make it virtually impossible to trace anything, much less recover it."

Stunned, Gale could only stare at him.

"It was so damned easy." Sax swore softly. His hands curled into fists as he scourged himself for eleven years of neglect. He should have been here. Someone should've been here to notice that Everette Hale, the family lawyer, was getting too old to keep up with things and too stubborn to let go. Olivia might or might not have been capable of understanding the complexity of the Evanshaw holdings.

As for his adopted stepbrother, Sax had no reason to believe that Jeff had ever matured much beyond what he'd been at fifteen—a wild kid with the sort of looks women would always find irresistible.

Richard had no longer been young when Sax had left home. It was entirely possible that he'd grown negligent. It took a strong and capable man to ride herd on someone as shrewd as Benton, and from the way things were looking, the shell game had started within days of Richard's stroke, while the whole household was still in an uproar.

"What are you going to do now?" Gale asked dully. To her own ears her voice sounded as if it came from a distance. None of this was really happening. She'd wake up in a little while and discover that it had all been a dream.

Sax raked a hand through his hair. He looked tortured. "I wish to hell I knew, Gale. Save what can be saved, try to catch up with that thieving scum, I guess. I don't know if there's anything left. Oh, there's the house, of course, and some rental properties around the state. I do know that it's my responsibility to salvage whatever I can without letting Dad find out what's going on. Whatever happens, his health comes first."

She couldn't think of a thing to say. More than ever she felt as if she didn't belong here. "Sax, I'm so sorry. If there's anything I can do..." She let it drop. Hadn't she done enough? What she'd stolen was a pittance compared to what Benton had evidently gotten away with.

All the same, she reminded herself, she was guilty of the same crime. It was merely a matter of degree. When it came to trust there was no gray areas, only black and white. You either trusted or you didn't.

And Sax couldn't.

Chapter Eleven

Saxon finished off his double bourbon and stared at the typed message. That was almost the worst of all—the fact that she'd typed it as if it were a business letter.

> Under the circumstances, I think it would be better if I moved out. Until I get settled somewhere, I would like your permission to continue to use the darkroom. I'll have it moved as soon as it's feasible.

As soon as it's feasible! What kind of language was that between two people who were in love and planning to be married? As soon as it's feasible indeed!

> The enclosed key is for the locked drawer in Richard's room at Laurel Hill. I had the lock installed after his first tape player was stolen.

There's nothing in it except for a new tape player,
several tapes of march music, his glasses and
bridgework. Play him a tape now and then—I
think he likes it. Emma Matlock in the office has
a duplicate key.

Sax poured himself another drink. He'd regret it
later, the way he'd regretted last night's drinks when
he'd wakened with a blinding headache this morning.
But when he'd come downstairs in search of something to wash down his pills and found instead the envelope with his name written in Gale's distinctive
scribble, he'd forgotten all about the damned headache.

The first page was short and to the point—instructions, for the most part, on managing the household
affairs. As if that weren't bad enough, there was a
second page.

This is an accounting of everything I owe you
except for the loan. I'll go by the bank on Monday and find out how much you deposited and
make arrangements to return it to you as quickly
as possible, at the bank's rate of interest. I've attached the receipts for the things I sold. I think
Mr. Crump had buyers for a few of the items. I'll
call and ask him to hold anything he has left until I can arrange to buy them back, and you have
my word that I'll repay you as soon as possible
for the things that have already left his hands.
There's no way I know of to make up for the sen-
timental value. I'm truly sorry, Saxon. At the
time I sold those things, I thought I was doing it
for the best of reasons.

The best of reasons. He could almost hear the words spoken in her soft, husky tones. She'd look him in the eye, too, integrity in every inch of that bewitching little body.

Damn! How could he have misread the situation so badly? It had been right there before his eyes from the very first—the conflict between concrete evidence versus his own instincts. Once again he'd made the mistake of believing the evidence! Once again, he'd misjudged the whole situation.

He wanted her back. He knew he'd have wanted her back if she'd been guilty as hell of wholesale larceny, but he was beginning to suspect that she'd been cleverly set up. She could have walked away when things first started falling apart. She could have joined that sister of hers in Italy.

Instead, she'd stayed behind and kept a leaky raft afloat any way she could for the single remaining passenger, an old man in a nursing home who was unable to offer his thanks, much less his support.

So what now? Track her down and apologize? "Come back, darling, all is forgiven—you're not quite the thief I thought you were?"

Sure, and have her slam the door in his face. For someone who'd been through as much as she had, Gale had more pride than the law allowed. For that reason, if for no other, he had to get to the bottom of this mess before he went after her. The Evanshaw clan owed her more than they could ever repay. At least he could find out the truth and offer her that.

In a motel room on the outskirts of Asheville, Gale slipped off her shoes and propped her feet on the bed while she composed another list. The plastic veneer table beside her was littered with lists. She was good at making them, but not so good at remembering where they were when she needed them. It was not at all unusual for her to rush into a store and come to a dead halt, wondering what on earth it was that she'd come in to buy.

"All right, we'll take one thing at a time," she announced to the row of stuffed toys at the head of the bed.

Rolling the ballpoint pen absently between her fingers, she stared at the patch of sky visible through the jumble of signs and trucks and power lines outside. Between the drink machines just outside her door, the cleaning supply room just beyond and the ceaseless roar of the interstate, she was beginning to see why she'd been able to get the room at bargain rates. After a day and a half, she was considering investing the few dollars she had left in a pair of industrial earplugs.

It was close to the restaurant, however, and until she could find something better that she could afford, it would have to do. The job was the most important thing, and with her singular lack of training, she'd been lucky to land one so quickly.

It had been Enid who'd inadvertently given her the idea of looking for work as a waitress. In the right sort of place, the tips would be good, and her daylight hours would be free to finish her book. She'd be able to subsist, and possibly even make a start at paying back a few debts.

If nothing went wrong, her publisher should have the completed manuscript and photos for *The Bridge to Golly's House* within two weeks. Then, *if* the book was accepted, and *if* the editor acted promptly, she might begin looking for an advance within another six weeks. Not a very large sum, but enough to pay back the rest of what she owed Saxon.

Saxon.

With a deep, shuddering sigh that expressed more hopelessness than hope, Gale gave in to the tide of feelings she'd been holding back ever since she'd packed three suitcases, a camera case, her typewriter, and two Hefty bags, and quietly left Saxon Hall.

He'd still been in the study. The light had slivered out beneath the door, and she'd heard the clink of bottle against glass when she'd retrieved her coat from the hall closet. It had taken all the restraint she possessed to keep from dashing into the study and throwing herself at him, begging him to forget what she'd done and try to learn to trust her enough to give her a second chance.

Of course she hadn't. Stealing from the man she loved had stripped her of most of her pride and self-respect. Accepting more of his charity would have finished her off.

With only a few hours of on-the-job training during the slack period, Gale threw all her energies into her work at Stumpy's Steak House. She blessed Enid again for mentioning the fact that she'd earned enough waiting tables to put herself through school.

After the first day, she wished Enid had also mentioned the importance of wearing comfortable shoes. Her second night on the job, she'd hobbled into her room shortly before midnight after serving a victory dinner for a local football team and their girlfriends. She'd barely made it to the bed before collapsing.

The next morning it had taken an hour's soaking in a tub of hot water to restore mobility to her feet. From the knees down, she'd felt as if she were one enormous ache.

Once she got accustomed to spending hours on her feet on thinly carpeted concrete floors, juggling heavy trays while she avoided tripping over out-thrust legs, bumping into projecting chairs, and dodging the over-friendly attentions of a few determined male diners, Gale was grateful for the fact that she was alternately too busy and too exhausted to waste much time thinking about Saxon and what might have been.

The first thing she'd done was to drive back to Shepparton and finish shooting the last scene for her book. It had been easy enough to avoid Sax, knowing that he usually spent the morning hours visiting Richard and sometimes dropped by again in the late afternoon.

Gale took advantage of his absences to use the darkroom, working much more efficiently than she normally did, but there was no way of hurrying the actual developing and printing processes. She felt almost furtive as she let herself in the utility room door, raced through her work and crept out again, keeping a careful watch for the Jeep.

Not until she was safely back at the motel did she relax enough to analyze each picture, determining what went wrong with the bad shots and gloating over the good ones. She carefully avoided drifting off on creative tangents, pondering the possibility of a whole series of Golly books. There would be time enough for dreaming when her first book had been officially accepted.

It was five days after she'd left Saxon Hall that Gale came home after work to discover a familiar-looking Jeep parked in front of her unit. She'd driven the short distance to work because it had been raining hard at four-thirty when she'd left the motel.

It still was. And now someone had parked in her space. Someone who drove the same model Jeep that Sax did—the same shade of blue, with the same streak of lighter blue on the door where the paint had been touched up, but never finished.

There was no mistaking the figure that slid out from the driver's side and hurried over to her car. Even with the sheepskin collar of his leather jacket turned up and his face turned down against the driving rain, Gale would have recognized Saxon anywhere. A wet, cold wind whipped at his jeans, outlining his powerful masculine body. He reached out for her door and yanked it open.

"You planning on roosting here all night?"

"How'd you find me?"

"Do you really want me to risk drowning while I tell you about the friend of a friend who works for the highway patrol and has had every trooper in three counties looking for your car? It's a damned good thing you drive something so highly visible."

Gale stared at him helplessly. Rain was dripping down his nose, gleaming on his shoulders. He looked tired and cold, mad as hell—and perfectly magnificent.

She pulled the keys out of the ignition and braced herself for whatever he had in mind. She didn't know which was worse—seeing him again, or never seeing him again. However, once she left the car she didn't have time to consider it when he followed her inside the motel room.

"How long have you been here?" she asked, dropping her damp coat inside the door. Until she saw him staring at her, she'd forgotten she was still wearing her uniform. She was still getting used to the black stockings, the short, black skirt and the tiny bibbed apron worn over a deeply slashed blouse. On someone like Enid, the amount of cleavage revealed would have been cataclysmic. On Gale, it was hardly enough to cast a shadow.

"Long enough," Sax said gruffly. "Go put on some clothes, that thing's indecent."

Gale bristled. "It's a uniform. There's nothing indecent about it."

"You enjoy prancing around in next to nothing? Pardon me all to hell and back, lady, I thought you might have found it embarrassing." His tone was heavily laced with sarcasm.

"I don't prance, I *work*," she stressed. "So does every other waitress I know. If you find my uniform offensive, then you have my permission to leave."

Sax's gaze moved over her, missing nothing, from the ridiculous patch of ruffles and ribbons pinned on top of her upswept hair to the sensible, rubber-soled shoes she'd insisted on wearing in spite of having been advised that the higher her heels, the higher her tips. Especially on Saturday night.

"We need to talk." He continued to glower at her from just inside the door, and Gale moved instinctively to the other side of the tiny room.

"I don't think so," she said.

"You didn't seriously believe I'd let you disappear with nothing but a stiff little note that read like an IOU, did you?"

"It *was* an IOU."

"You don't owe me anything! Why won't you trust me to—"

"Trust! You want to talk about trust?" If she sounded bitter, it was because she felt bitter. Bitter and hurt, and unwilling to give an inch for fear of losing the little ground she'd gained. "What do you want, my signature in blood? Why did you have to come after me, anyway? Did you really think I was running out on a debt? Maybe I should have changed my name—oh yes, I should have remembered to have my car repainted and to muddy the license plate. I'm such a slow learner!"

His look was deadly, but when he finally spoke, Saxon's voice was calm. Almost expressionless.

"Several things have happened since last weekend," he said, the flexing of his jaw the only sign of the anger that had flared between them a moment before. "In case you're still interested in my father's progress—"

"You know I am," Gale said quickly.

He'd never doubted her genuine concern, not since the first time he'd discovered how many hours she'd spent at Laurel Hill, how she'd brought tapes and a player, and then bought a new tape player for him when the first one had been stolen.

No, he'd never doubted her caring, not even when he'd suspected the worst of her.

God, how could he have been so blind! And how could he convince her that his coming after her had nothing to do with the fact that he now knew her only crime had been trying to keep her balance after that pair of conniving thieves had pulled the rug out from under her feet?

Patience was the key. Patience, tact and caution. He'd use whatever means he had to get her back, because to do without her would be unthinkable. But he had to move carefully or she'd bolt again. And this time he might not be lucky enough to find her so easily. "Gale, I've talked to the doctors about taking Dad back home."

Gale's mouth fell open. "Home? To Saxon Hall? When? How can you? Won't he need special care?" She dropped down onto the foot of the bed, sending dozens of neatly stacked photographs cascading to the floor unnoticed.

"Any questions?" A smile tugged at the corners of his mouth for an instant. "The doctor seems to think his chances of recovery might be improved by bringing him back to familiar surroundings. He'd have round-the-clock nurses, of course, at least for the time being. They're trying him on liquids this week. So far, it looks promising."

"I can't believe it," Gale said under her breath. A shoe hit the floor as she curled one foot under her. "A few weeks ago, I was wondering if he'd ever respond to anything again. Then his hand moved under mine, and now . . ."

For the first time, she seemed to notice that Sax was still standing just inside the door, his heavy jacket gleaming wetly. Damp jeans clung to his lean, powerful legs, and his boots were darkly saturated.

He moved restlessly. "Yeah—well, according to the experts, nobody has too many answers as to what goes on in a case like this. No two are alike. There'll be some permanent damage, naturally. Probably quite a lot. It might be years before we even know the extent of it."

"Sax, stop hovering, you make me nervous. Take off your jacket and sit down. I'll make us some instant coffee—I have one of those gadgets you stick in a cup to heat water." It's almost as though nothing had ever happened between us, Gale thought. We're like two strangers joined only by our concern for a mutual friend.

Saxon crossed the room to drape his wet jacket over a straight chair, and Gale brushed past him on her way to the lavatory. Every cell in her body clamored out an alarm.

"Excuse me," he muttered, stepping out of the way. "Not much room in here."

"Sorry. Next time I'll ask for the presidential suite." She couldn't help but remember another motel room, where they'd shared a bed, shared their worries and consoled each other in a silent bond of understanding.

He sent her a withering look, which she ignored.

"I'm sorry I don't have anything else to offer you. I eat at the restaurant—one of the perks of being a waitress." Her smile faltered, and she set about making coffee.

Dwarfing the shabby room with his presence, Sax moved to the head of the bed and propped up one of the toys that had toppled over unnoticed. "The motley crew, all present and accounted for, I see." He accepted the mug, took a sip and tried not to grimace, and Gale thought longingly of the delicious coffee brewed with water from Saxon Hall's deep well.

"And what are these?" He picked up one of the photos that had slithered to the floor. It was one of the Biltmore batch, showing Golly, his ears flying in the wind and his Velcro eyes round as saucers as he clung to the top of a boulder and gazed down on the wonderful palace he'd inadvertently stumbled upon.

Sax reached for another photograph. Then another. He went back to the first one, and then he laid them all down and turned to Gale. "This is what you call dabbling? Why didn't you tell me?"

"Tell you what?" She felt as though she'd swallowed a big bite of steak without chewing.

"About these—about what you were doing with all those toys. What *are* you doing with them, anyway?" he added as an afterthought.

"Saxon, never mind about that. What about Richard? Have you engaged a nurse yet? Aggie Crews is my favorite, but of course that's up to you. You might want to consider a male nurse. And then there's Olivia. Were you able to get word to her yet?"

"Whoa, one thing at a time, honey."

The plastic coffee cup tilted alarmingly as Gale reacted to the careless endearment. Of course, it meant nothing, except as a sign that he was no longer actively hostile. She'd be a fool to start clutching at straws. "I want to know everything—is Olivia coming home? How did she sound? But give me a minute to change first, will you? I smell like fried onions."

There was nowhere to change but the bathroom, and that was hardly large enough to close the door with one person inside. Gale managed to dash cold water over her face, take down her hair and change into yellow corduroy jeans and a pale lavender sweater. Despite the few knocks she'd received in the process, she felt considerably better.

"You look more like Easter morning than the week after Thanksgiving," Sax observed when she joined him a few minutes later.

"Most of my things are still packed, since I'm planning to move as soon as I find something more suitable." Something more affordable was more like it. "So many of the old rooming houses have hung out fancy Bed-and-Breakfast signs and adjusted their rates accordingly, that it's taking a little longer than I'd expected."

Suddenly aware of the way Sax was looking at her, as if he'd momentarily forgotten why he'd gone to the trouble of tracking her down, Gale's guard slipped another notch. "You were telling me about Richard," she reminded him. "I'm not sure how Mrs. McCrary's going to take the news. If it means more work, she might want more money."

"I suspect she's getting about three times what she's worth already. What did you pay her, anyway?"

Gale named a figure, and Sax swore under his breath. "That tipsy old pirate. She told me twice that much. In advance!"

"You have to be firm, Saxon. She tends to only do so much, so there's no point in expecting miracles, but she knows she's lucky to have a job at all." She finished her tasteless coffee and got rid of the cup. "It's Olivia I'm worried about," she said. "I'm not sure how she's going to react when she gets back home. One of the reasons she needed to get away in the first place was that being around sick people depresses her. Some people are like that, you know. It's really not their fault."

To Gale's amazement, Sax's eyes paled to a glacial shade of blue. "I wouldn't worry about Olivia's reaction," he said grimly. "As to her reasons for clearing out when she did, I doubt very seriously that depression was one of them, regardless of what she led you to believe."

"But you can't know that," Gale said quickly. She'd tried to deny her dislike of Jeff's mother for so long now that the defense came automatically. Still she'd been puzzled by Olivia's odd behavior too—the alternate spells of withdrawal and hyperactivity. It had been Olivia herself who'd told her that the psychiatrist she'd been seeing since Jeff's death had recommended the cruise as a remedy for depression.

"No, I can't," Sax said dryly, "but I can come pretty close to guessing. I've just discovered that the Olivia Evanshaw who's currently cruising through the Panama Canal is actually a woman named Martha Fleiderman. Ms. Fleiderman, it seems, was delighted to take over Olivia's reservations at the last minute for a fraction of the original cost."

He raked his fingers through his hair, leaving it standing on end, and it was all Gale could do to keep from reaching out to smooth it down again. Her body reacted instinctively, even with her mind caught up in what he was telling her. "But I don't understand how it could have happened. Or why," she persisted.

"I don't know all the answers. Not yet. The reservations were in Olivia's name, but the other woman would have had to use her own passport."

"That explains it, then," Gale said flatly, recalling her problems with the bank. "Reservations are made on computers, and anywhere you have computers, you have the potential for disaster. If this was a last-minute change, chances are it never got put into the computer. Or maybe they're both listed as passengers. Anything's possible in this age of new and improved bookkeeping."

"Could be. I just found out about the switch this morning when I tried to place a call through a marine operator."

"But Sax, I still don't understand. Why would Olivia change her mind and not even tell me? Are you *sure* there hasn't been an accident? Maybe this Fleidermouse woman stole the tickets, and—"

"Fleiderman."

"Whatever," she gestured impatiently. If just one more thing could go wrong, it probably had. From the day her mother-in-law had waved goodbye, it had been one thing after another. "Look, I don't know what's going on around here, but I'm beginning to think there's something seriously wrong. Besides Benton, I mean." Unconsciously, she began kneading the tender ball of her foot.

"Wrong!" Sax snorted. As if he could no longer contain the restless energy that seethed in him, he stood and began pacing.

Gale watched in silence. She felt as if she were being physically assaulted by his anger, by the turbulence just under the surface of his lean, hard body. If he didn't calm down and explain what this was all about, she was going to fly apart. "Would you please stop prowling?" she cried. "Whatever's on your mind, for goodness sake, speak out! If it's me you're still angry with, then just tell me so. You're making me sick!"

Thunderstruck, he stopped pacing to stare at her. "I make you *sick*?"

"Oh, for pity's sake, not *that* way," she exclaimed. "I just meant that I—well, I seem to be sort of—" She shook her head in defeat. How could she explain without getting herself in even deeper?

"Sick," Sax filled in for her.

"Well, can I help it if my stomach's tuned in to the same frequency your head happens to be broadcasting on? Don't ask me why, but when you're all churned up inside the way you are now, it makes me feel almost seasick." Her fingers worked frantically, kneading the sole of her right foot, as if the mere expenditure of physical energy could defuse the emotional time bomb ticking away inside her.

Sax was beside her in a moment. Leaning over, he cupped her face between his hands, forcing her to meet his eyes. "Gale, listen to me. Whatever happens, I want you to know that none of this is your fault. You're in no way to blame for whatever's going on, or for the way I happen to be feeling."

The tension that narrowed his eyes to hard sapphire slits seemed to drain away even as she watched. After what seemed an eternity, he smiled. Gale thought dazedly that it must be comparable to watching the sun come out after a forty-day rain.

"Correction," he said huskily. "You're very much responsible for the way I'm feeling right now."

"I am?" Her whisper was barely audible.

Easing down beside her, he replaced the fingers on her aching foot with his own warmer, stronger ones. "Is this where it hurts?"

"Mmm, right there." She gasped as he touched a particularly tender place. "I'm fine until that last hour. By the time I get home, I feel like I've been walking barefoot over a bed of coals."

"I remember feeling pretty much the same way after my first week of riding fence. Nine hours a day in a saddle that felt like it might have been designed by the Marquis de Sade."

"That made your feet hurt?"

"Relatively speaking, honey."

Gale had no idea how much tension had accumulated in her own body since she'd come home to find him waiting for her. On second thought, it had probably been accumulating ever since she'd driven away from Saxon Hall.

Or since that night nearly a month ago when she'd opened the door to find him standing on the doorstep.

Her shoulders drooped, and she sighed. "Better?" Sax murmured, and she nodded.

"I'd still like to have some idea of what's going on," she said after he'd worked on both feet, massaging away most of their soreness through the thin layer of black nylon. "If it's not too much trouble."

"Who wouldn't," Sax said whimsically. "You deserve to know, more than anyone else involved, but I'm afraid you're going to have to wait."

"For what?" Her lips barely moved. Somehow, she found herself lying back on the pillows, her head resting on one of Golly's plush ears.

Sax leaned over her, and she gave in to temptation and lifted her hand to smooth back the thick, soft hair that tumbled over his forehead. "So far, I've got one private investigator tracking down Tad Benton, another one trying to pick up Olivia's trail, a new law firm going over everything with a fine-tooth comb, and your friend Aggie from Laurel Hill is checking the house over to see what needs to be done before we bring Dad home."

Dizzy for more reasons than one, Gale blinked several times in rapid succession. "Is that all?"

"Not quite, but if you're going to keep on fluttering your eyelashes at me, it might be a while before we get around to the rest of it."

Chapter Twelve

It was almost like coming home, Gale thought a week later as she pulled up and parked in her usual spot outside the garage. After working out the minimum notice, finishing with a double shift, she felt an uncomfortable mixture of emotions. Besides being exhausted, she was surprisingly happy to be back. After the melodramatic way she'd crept out in the middle of the night, though, she was a bit embarrassed.

But two weeks of living in a cramped and noisy motel room was enough for anyone. At this point, she'd have been thrilled to move into Otis Pilky's barn.

The Jeep was missing, which meant that Sax was gone. It was almost a relief, Gale thought as she began carrying her bags into the utility room. She'd get them all inside, and then haul them to her room, and hopefully she'd have time to wash up and change into something a little fresher before he got back.

She'd just dragged the last of the lot from the trunk when Sax pulled up beside her. "You should have waited to let me carry that stuff in for you," he reproached, relieving her of the largest suitcase. Filled with shoes, photos and manuscript, it weighed a ton.

"Where were you when I was carrying trays full of steak dinners on cast iron grilling plates and heavy pitchers of beer?" Gale grabbed her camera case in one hand and her portable typewriter in the other and followed him inside.

"Upstairs, take your pick," he said when she would have turned into the west wing.

"Oh, but—"

"Aggie and Dad are already installed on the first floor. Your suite was perfect for them. I didn't think you'd mind."

"No, I don't mind. Whatever's convenient." Gale shrugged. She warned herself not to take anything for granted. She was here because Sax had said he needed her, that Richard would need her. Beyond that, he'd actually said very little.

"Good. Dad's settled in even better than we'd hoped. A therapist comes out once a day, and Aggie's got a list of names if we need additional help. So far she thinks she can handle it alone."

Gale tried not to stare too openly at the tall, tanned man in the close-fitting jeans and flannel shirt, but she was so desperately hungry for the sight of him. A week ago he'd left shortly after she'd given her word that she would quit her job and move back to Saxon Hall. Since then, she'd heard nothing at all from him.

Naturally, he'd have been busy, with all the investigations going on, and all the preparations for bringing Richard home. But none of the excuses she'd invented had helped her get to sleep at night, no matter how tired she'd been.

"Sounds like everything's all taken care of," she said with determined cheerfulness.

Taking the typewriter case and tucking it under his arm, Sax started up the stairs. "Nothing's taken care of," he said over his shoulder. "Mrs. McCrary quit day before yesterday, and so far the agency hasn't been able to come up with a replacement. What happened to all the housekeepers?"

"They either retired or got better jobs, I guess."

"Yeah, well... Aggie's been pinch-hitting in the kitchen, but she's a lousy cook. Besides, it's not what I hired her for."

Gale lifted her chin fractionally, but she made no comment. She didn't begin to understand all that went on behind those enigmatic blue eyes of his, but if he needed her help, he had it. She owed him that much, and more.

Moving with the lean grace that was so typical of him, Sax took the stairs easily in spite of the load he carried. "The room next to mine's been aired out recently. It's the one Enid used, remember?"

Gale pushed past him and stopped at the far end of the hall. "This one'll do just fine. In case I need to do any typing at night, I wouldn't want to disturb you." And the *last* thing I need to help me keep my wits about me is a connecting door to your bedroom, she added silently.

Ignoring his quick flash of irritation at her choice, she said, "If you'll put those in here, I'll get the rest of my stuff from the utility room."

"Don't bother," he said grimly, and Gale nodded. Round one to her.

Waiting, she tried out the mattress on the high narrow bed, bouncing once or twice. As far as she knew, the room hadn't been used in years. The heavy cherry furniture, with its rather crudely carved pineapple motif, was dusty—hardly surprising, considering the housekeeper's aversion to climbing stairs. The pink-and white-sprigged wallpaper was rather charming, but the two narrow windows, with their limp white curtains, overlooked nothing more picturesque than a corner of the garage, the sagging roof of the potting shed and the compost pit.

"Well, what did you expect, you goose?" she said out loud. "A whoop-de-do homecoming celebration? That Saxon would sweep you off your feet and carry you over the threshold? *You're* the one who agreed to come back, *you're* the one who picked out this room, and for once, you showed a little common sense, so quit moping!"

It was that darned fiction-oriented mind of hers! Even as a child she'd given it a workout, inventing all these wildly exotic reasons why she'd been shunted off on whatever relative would have her. She'd imagined that she was actually the child of her favorite aunt, and that on her eighteenth birthday, Aunt Polly would clasp her to her Shalimar-scented bosom and "reveal all."

Nor had she outgrown her weakness for happy endings. It hadn't helped when her own sister had married a handsome storybook prince and gone off to live in a palace, never mind that the palatial plumbing usually didn't work. Her fairy-tale dreams had her flying blind in a rosy cloud of romance when she'd impulsively agreed to elope with Jeff.

She'd been flying blind when she'd fallen in love with Sax too, she admitted with painful self-honesty. She'd taken it for granted that because he'd made love to her, it followed that he loved her. And if he loved her, could the inevitable happy ending be far away?

"Oh, God, Gale, you are truly a lost cause!" She slipped off the bed and yanked open a suitcase, trying to concentrate on unpacking. But unpacking wasn't the sort of chore that required much thought.

All right, so Jeff had married her because he thought it would please Richard, not because she was any dream come true. And Sax had made love to her because she was willing and available—and obviously besotted with him. It had been a simple matter of biology on his part. He hadn't needed to make any promises because her flaky little brain had already sketched in the whole scenario, up to and including the traditional happy ending. Now he'd asked her here because he needed someone to run his house, and she'd come trotting dutifully back.

Why did she always have to be the means to a man's end? Was it too much to expect to be appreciated because she was a reasonably attractive woman, with a degree of talent and a modicum of intelligence? Was that too much to ask?

"Where do you want the motley crew?" Sax inquired as he appeared in the doorway with a Hefty bag and the last of her luggage. "You're sure they're housebroken?"

"Yes, but their fleas aren't," she snapped. "I'll try to see that they don't roam too far." She couldn't quite meet his eyes. He was being thoroughly decent, and she was being thoroughly childish. It was hardly his fault she had this unfortunate penchant for confusing fact with fiction.

"Gale, is everything all right?" Sax asked, suddenly serious.

She concentrated hard on arranging a blouse on a padded hanger. "Everything's just lovely, thank you. Would you like me to start on dinner now, or should I consult with Aggie first?"

If he'd been a fire-breathing dragon, she'd have been incinerated on the spot. "Would you mind telling me what the hell that's supposed to mean?" he asked in grimly measured tones.

Gale lifted her head just a fraction. "You need a hearing aid?"

"No, I need an interpreter!" He was beside her instantly, his fingers biting into her shoulders. "What's the matter with you, Gale? If you didn't want to come back, why did you bother?"

"I think that's pretty obvious, don't you?" She looked pointedly down at his hands.

He ignored the look. "Nothing's obvious! Not one damned thing! Since the first day I came back here, I've been running around like a rat in a maze. It's been one wrong turn after another."

"One dead end after another, you mean."

"If you prefer. But there's a way out of this maze, Gale. I'm finally on the right track." The pressure of his hands on her shoulders eased slightly, and then, as if he'd only just noticed what he was doing, his hands fell away. "Bear with me a little longer, Gale. There'll be plenty of time for—"

From somewhere down the hall, a phone shrilled. They stared at each other, not touching, not speaking. It rang again, and Gale stepped back. "You'd better get it, it might be important."

While Sax answered the phone, Gale unpacked another suitcase, moving mechanically between bed and dresser and closet. She hated unpacking even worse than she hated packing, yet sometimes it seemed as if she'd done little else in her life.

The low murmur of Sax's voice came to her as she lifted out the gray wool jersey dress she'd worn to dinner with him the night at the Hunting Ridge Club. He'd been talking for quite a while, it seemed, when suddenly he was there again, filling the doorway, filling her eyes—and her heart.

"It's for you," he said. "Your sister."

Gale let the lid of her pullman case fall shut as she stared at him. "Susan?"

"You have more than one sister living in Italy?"

"Susan!" she cried, pushing past him to dash down the hall.

Three days later they were still arguing over the impending visit. "They can stay at a hotel," Gale said, as she'd said countless times before.

"I've already invited them to stay here."

"That's totally unreasonable, and you know it! Especially under the circumstances." Richard had settled in very well, and Aggie already seemed like one of the family, but the household was still far from being back to normal. "Saxon, I can't see why you're doing this to me. Are you deliberately trying to make me uncomfortable?''

They were hanging the paintings Sax had collected to replace the China Trade group. "Up an inch—too much, down a hair. Okay, mark the spot."

Gale placed a light pencil mark at the top of the frame, and Sax measured the distance between the top of the frame and the apex of the wire hanger. He nailed a hook into the paneling, hung the contemporary impressionistic landscape and stepped back to admire the effect.

"I like it. You know, the color really does something for this room, doesn't it? There's such a thing as getting in a rut."

Gale jammed the pencil in her hair and planted her fists on her hips. "Did you hear a single word I've said?"

"Yep."

"Well?"

"House party."

"What?" she screeched.

"I said, *house party*. That's what you were talking about, isn't it? I told you I was listening." He reached for another of the three paintings left to be hung and eyed the pale patches on the paneling, and Gale chewed her lip and wondered if it was all a deliberate plot to drive her finally and irredeemably around the bend.

It was working.

They finished hanging the last canvas, and Gale was forced to agree with him that the room looked immensely better. The cool blues and greens of the nautical paintings had been just right with the faded blue and gray rugs and the leather furniture, but the richer blue of the familiar peaks, with splashes of colorful rhododendron and laurel in the foreground, created a completely different feeling.

"The new rugs'll be delivered tomorrow. You'll have to help me decide what goes where. Interior decorating's never been my forte." Sax sprawled in one of the armchairs, one leg thrown over the arm. His sleeves were rolled up, and there was a faint sheen of perspiration under the haze of dark hair on his muscular forearm.

"You seem to be doing all right."

"Blind luck, honey, blind luck." He winked at her, and her mood deteriorated further.

"If that's all you need, then I'll go on up. If I'm going to have the floors buffed and ready by the time the truck comes, I'll need to start early."

Sax watched her leave, her back as straight as a pine sapling. He sighed, got up and poured himself a drink, and then ignored it. So much for Plan B.

Plan A had been to enlist her help in getting his father settled in. He'd figured her natural concern for Richard would hold her there until he could steal a few hours away from the godawful mess Benton had left behind.

What he hadn't figured on was that she'd insist on working out her notice first. Nor had he realized that he'd be so damned tied up. Between getting things set up here at home and flying to London after a report that Tad Benton had been seen there with a woman answering to Olivia Evanshaw's description, he hadn't even had time to call her, much less try to get through that barricade she'd thrown up around herself.

And now Plan B was foundering.

Sweeping Gale irrevocably into the middle of his life had been Plan B. Crude, but effective—he'd gotten the idea from the way they herded cattle into a loading chute at Steppin' Creek.

Actually, the idea had first come to him when Susan had called. It seemed that her husband had to make a quick business trip to the States, and Susan had thought it would be perfect opportunity to visit her sister.

The whole house party idea had grown out of Susan's call that first night. When Enid had phoned to say she might pop in for a coffee on her way back home, Sax had insisted she break the long drive west with another short visit.

She'd agreed, promising to tell them all about her shirttail cousin, Willis Boone, who hadn't lived up to his billing.

Jay's flying east had been a stroke of genius. Sax had felt obligated from the first to keep his partner apprised of the situation, as it had a direct bearing on how long he'd have to be away from the ranch. He'd been slightly less forthcoming about the way he was beginning to feel about leaving home again. That would have to be worked out later, after things had settled out here.

"Enid'll be dropping in for a few days on her way back to Guymon," he'd mentioned several days ago when Jay had called about an offer he'd had for a strip of land that fronted on highway 64.

"How'd things go with that cousin of hers in Richmond?"

"Didn't, as far as I could tell. She'll be driving west alone."

"Damned shame. Long drive for a woman."

"Yeah," Sax had agreed, grinning broadly. "I'd offer to help her out, but there's no telling when I'll be able to leave here. The way things are beginning to shape up, I might have to renegotiate our deal to be fair to you."

"Now don't make any hasty moves, Dude. No reason we can't carry on same's ever, with me doin' all the work an' you settin' back on your south end telling me how it ought to be done."

"You know, the trouble with you, old man, is that you've been spending too much time nursing that last bunch of polled Herefords we bought. You're beginning to think like—"

"Polled Hereford, huh," the older man had muttered, referring to the herd of dehorned beef cattle they were fattening for market. "You callin' me hornless?"

Sax had tipped back his chair and propped his booted feet on the hearth. "I only meant that you might be spending too much time with the boys. Maybe you just need a break." And then he proceeded to tell him about the small house party planned for the following week.

By that time, Sax had already been in too deep to back out.

Aggie had been horrified. "Do you have any idea what all this carousing could do to your father? He's making progress now, but if I'd known you had any such thing in mind, I'm not sure I'd have recommended letting him come home."

"Just close friends and family, Aggie, and only for a few days. I could hardly ask Gale's sister and brother-in-law to stay at Sugar Ridge Inn, and driv-

ing back and forth between here and Asheville's out of
the question.''

"I hope you plan to get some extra help in," the
nurse had snapped. "For all Gale's willingness, she
almost poisoned us the other night with that French
thing she cooked up.''

"It was pretty bad," he'd been forced to admit.
"But the fried chicken was great. And she's had all she
could do interviewing housekeepers and helping me
get things back in shape around here.''

"She works too hard," the nurse observed sharply.
"And she doesn't smile enough, either. Something's
eating at her, if you ask me.''

"Something's eating at all of us, Aggie," Sax had
admitted. He'd grown fond of the fierce little woman
who guarded her patient so zealously. "Maybe that's
all the more reason for bringing in a few new faces.
They're nice people, all of them.''

With the possible exception of the ice princess from
the Italian palazzo, he added silently. She'd sounded
friendly enough over the phone, but he'd withhold
judgment until after he'd met her. "I promise you,
Aggie, if any of this disturbs Dad, I'll clear the lot of
'em out of here. It ought to bring back a few old
memories, though," he mused, his eyes softening
noticeably. "Whenever things got a little too stuffy
around here, my mother used to throw a party. It always seemed to help bring Dad out of himself for a
few hours.''

"You old sonofagun, so this is why you come east
and stuck tighter'n stink on a polecat!'' The two men
embraced, and Jay slapped his younger partner on the
back a few times and stepped back to admire the newly

decorated foyer. He looked sincerely impressed as he took in the large oil landscape Sax and Gale had selected from an Asheville gallery to complement the richly patterned rug.

Gale, having hurriedly dressed in a yellow sweater dress after helping the new cook learn her way around the kitchen, came downstairs in time to see the two men discussing the painting.

This was Jay Mathis? This attractive man in the trim Western-cut suit of palest gray, with the white Stetson topping his weathered face? He wasn't at all what she'd expected. The one time she'd spoken to him on the phone, when he'd called and Sax had been out, he'd sounded like a tobacco-chewing, suspender-snapping refugee from a grade B Western.

"You must be Jackson Mathis," she said, descending the last few steps with her hand extended.

"Gale, this is Jay," Sax informed her. "Jay, I'd like you to meet—"

"The angel on top of the Christmas tree," the cowboy completed. Sweeping off his hat, he bent over her hand in a gesture that brought Gale to the verge of laughter for what seemed the first time in days. These past few weeks, she'd hardly had time to breathe, much less to laugh.

"Jay, I'm delighted to meet you in person. Has Sax shown you your room yet?"

"I was about to—" Sax began, when Jay broke in.

"Little angel, you can put me anywhere you want to, but first let me tell you, if this Dude don't appreciate you, why then you come on back to Oklahoma with me, and I'll show you how a *real* man treats his womenfolk."

At a strangled sound from Sax, Gale turned a coolly questioning look on him. She still hadn't come to terms with his reason for asking her back, but she was working on it. After this weekend was over, she'd have come close to paying back whatever she owed him. With interest!

Turning to Gale, Sax said dryly, "I'm not sure if that's his Slim Pickens or his Hoss Cartwright, but he's usually harmless enough. It's only when he gets started on his Rambo act that you have to worry."

"Let me show you where to put your bag, Jay," Gale suggested, leading the way upstairs. Sax followed, and she fancied she could feel his gaze on her back. But then, she'd fancied a lot of things since he'd come into her life. She was trying her best to cut back on fancying.

Susan and Tonio were next to arrive. Unfortunately, it was while Gale was out mailing her manuscript. She'd have carried it every step of the way to New York and delivered it by hand if she'd thought it would do any good, but she had to be content with muttering a few incantations, saying a few prayers, and sending it first-class, enclosed in a self-addressed stamped envelope.

As she rounded the curve in the driveway, she noticed the extra car. The Jeep was usually parked outside now, and Aggie's red Ford was in its usual place. Jay had flown into Asheville and taken a cab to Saxon Hall so the rented Chrysler must belong to...

"Susan!" Gale screamed, throwing herself out of the car and into the arms of the tall, obviously pregnant woman who'd come out to greet her.

They talked for what seemed like hours, catching up, getting reacquainted, touching on past tragedies and future prospects. Susan was glowingly happy, and Gale brushed over questions about her relationship with Saxon and talked instead of her hopes for the manuscript she'd just mailed and her plans for another book.

Tonio was as charming as ever, although he was a little shorter and a little more plump than she remembered. He was openly delighted at meeting a genuine American cowboy, and Jay played the part to the hilt.

Just as they sat down to dinner that evening, Enid arrived. Tonio's sparkling eyes widened almost comically as she dragged a chair up to the table and squeezed in between Gale and Jay. "What are you doing here, you ugly ol' buzzard? Are you following me?" she asked the beaming Westerner.

Turning to Gale, she rolled her eyes. "Honey, you know that cousin I was telling you about? Well, that man's elevated boring to a fine art. If I could've hung around long enough, I'd have patented him as a cure for insomnia." She accepted the plate and utensils from the housekeeper, smiling her thanks, and helped herself to a slice of country cured ham without pausing. "From Italy, you say? Now there's a place I'd like to visit. I've heard the Italian men know how to make a woman feel appreciated."

Saxon was obviously amused by the redhead's flamboyant style, and Tonio was openly enchanted. Gale noted with interest that Jay had edged closer until his chair was actually scraping against Enid's. Susan was the last to thaw, but not even she could hold out for long.

"Will you be staying long, Miss—uh, Enid?"

"Just long enough to rinse out my pantyhose and talk this ol' turkey here into drivin' me back home.

How 'bout it, Jay, think you can handle the horse-power?'' She waited just long enough for the cattle-man to turn fiery red before explaining to Susan, ''I've got this little Mercedes sports car, y'see, and when a man's used to driving a pickup truck…'' She shrugged expressively. Sax chuckled, Tonio grinned, and Jay swore and then begged the ladies' pardon.

They lingered over coffee and brandy, talking com-fortably. If Gale grew quieter as the evening pro-gressed, no one seemed to notice. It'd been a long, exciting day, and with Tonio leaving for New York in the morning only to return in two days to take Susan back to Florence, and Jay and Enid talking of getting off the next day as well, there was little time to con-centrate on her own plans.

After dinner they adjourned to the study, where hickory and apple logs crackled on the hearth, the men settling on one side of the room with cigars and bour-bon, and the three women taking the sofa. Gale had a fleeting image of similar gatherings in the future—the three couples, older, grayer, fitting comfortably to-gether in spite of the dissimilarity of backgrounds.

Gale forced her attention back to the discussion of Italian fashions, pretending an interest she scarcely felt. This was no time to start dreaming again. She might blend fact with fantasy in her work, but in real life, the two were worlds apart.

Seated across the room, Saxon nursed his bourbon and studied the three women. It was hardly surprising that he'd mistaken Gale for her sister at first. The re-semblance was striking, the main difference being that Susan was taller, older, and considerably more so-phisticated. It hadn't taken him long to realize that what he'd taken for haughtiness all those years ago had been partly shyness and partly an innate reserve.

Gale, on the other hand, was much more spontaneous, an intriguing mixture of strength and vulnerability, of pride and passion. Unfortunately, she'd deliberately built a wall around herself the minute she'd walked into the house again, and so far, he hadn't been able to reach her.

He wasn't sure what she thought she had to protect herself against, but he'd broached that wall once, and he would again. He'd *be* her wall, dammit, if she'd only let him!

Tonio got off early the next morning, and Jay and Enid departed a few hours later, declaring they had a long road ahead of them.

Gale rather suspected the road might be even longer than they thought, but only time would tell. She regretted that she wouldn't be in a position to find out whether or not that budding friendship ever blossomed and bore fruit.

Susan went up to bed soon after dinner. After conferring briefly with the housekeeper, Gale was ready to follow suit when Saxon waylaid her at the foot of the stairs.

"Come with me to see Dad. Aggie says you've been neglecting him lately."

Gale bristled defensively. "I'd hardly call it neglect. I saw him just this morning." The truth was, she'd been trying to wean herself from everything connected with the Evanshaws—even that was a painful business.

"Just kidding, Gale. Come along, we'll sit with him for a few minutes."

As they slipped into the room that had once been Gale's, Aggie moved immediately to stand beside her patient, one capable hand on his shoulder. "We've been reminiscing about the war," she said with a side-long glance at the white-haired man in the navy silk pajamas. "I served as a nurse in the Pacific theater."

Both Sax and Gale stared at her. To their knowledge, Richard had not spoken a word in nearly three months. They looked at each other, at Richard and back at Aggie, who laughed.

"Oh, there are ways of communicating, especially when you've been at it as long as I have. We've been going over Dick's scrapbooks."

"Scrapbooks?" Saxon repeated. After only the briefest hesitation, he crossed the room and took his father's withered hand in his tanned and strong one. In spite of his smile, it occurred to Gale that there was almost a wariness about his expression. "Dad, if I'd known you were wanting to talk over your days in the service, I'd have told you about how seasick I was the first time I went out on a deep-water cruise after boot camp."

Aggie grinned. "Dick says, if you'd bothered to ask, he would've warned you that Evanshaws always take awhile to get their sea legs."

Gale, seeing the emotion darkening Sax's eyes, edged toward the door. There was an undercurrent here she didn't understand, something between father and son. She didn't belong here.

"Gale, where are you slipping off to?" Aggie demanded. "Dick wants to know if you still have that tape of the Boston Pops doing Sousa."

"He does?" Bewildered, Gale edged closer to the bedside, which brought her closer to Sax, as well.

"Sure—I think it must be in with some of my tapes. I'll get it now."

This time there was a distinct change of expression on the face of the bedridden man. "No?" she murmured. "Then what—"

"I think I know what Dad wants." Sax slipped his arm around her waist and drew her against his side. "What about it, Dad, shall we keep her? She's something of a runt, and a distinct hazard in the kitchen, but I've sort of gotten attached to her."

Laughing, Gale muttered something rude under her breath, and was rewarded by a tremulous smile from the man who had not, to her knowledge, smiled since he'd been stricken.

Richard's lips moved, but no sound came forth. His smile was swiftly replaced by a look of unmistakable frustration, and Aggie moved around the bed to stand at his other side. All eyes were on the older man as he began to make feeble motions with the third finger of his right hand.

"Your signet ring?" Aggie interpreted, and Richard nodded very slightly.

Saxon gripped Gale's hand with crushing force. She could feel his growing tension radiating almost as a physical force.

"Dad—are you sure?" he asked huskily.

There was no need for an interpreter. Blazing blue eyes held faded ones of the same hue for what seemed an eternity. Gale's vision blurred, and she lifted her face to stare at an oak framed cheval glass.

It was Saxon who slipped the ring from his father's finger, a ring worn smooth by generations of wearers. He straightened again, holding the ring between thumb and forefinger as if awaiting further instructions.

"I think he must want you to put it on," Gale said softly.

It was Aggie who interpreted Richard's feeble movements this time. "He wants *you*," she said, looking directly at Gale, "to put it on Saxon's finger."

Gale stepped back, but not before hearing the sharp intake of Saxon's breath. "Aggie, I don't think—" she began.

"Dad, I think I know what you want, but that'll require two rings, won't it?"

Richard smiled and closed his eyes. Gale and Saxon waited, but the elderly man was obviously exhausted.

With a smile of apparent satisfaction, Aggie pulled the sheet higher over his chest and nodded toward the door. "He's worn out after all that. He'll sleep for several hours now," she said quietly, ushering the other two outside and following them out into the hall.

Saxon, looking unnaturally pale, still held the ring as if he weren't quite sure what to do with it—or himself. He looked almost in shock.

Gale glanced at the ring and then quickly looked away. She'd been both touched and embarrassed by Richard's gesture—or by Aggie's interpretation of it—but she had to find some way to let Saxon know that she didn't expect him to marry her just because he thought it might please his father. They'd probably been mistaken about the whole thing, anyway. Nothing had actually been said, it had only been a change of expressions. It could've meant anything—or nothing.

"Look, I'd better collect the cups and glasses from the study and then go on up. I'll see you in the morning," she said, the words directed at neither of them in particular.

"I'll catch a nap while Dick dozes then," Aggie replied. "Good night, you two."

While Gale stacked the few cups and glasses on a tray to take out to the kitchen, Sax banked the fire and adjusted the screen. "Don't go yet, Gale," he said.

"Oh, I—it's late, Sax. I'd better clear away this mess and—"

"Leave it for what's her name. I didn't bring you back home to wash dishes."

"I wasn't going to wash them." China and crystal clattered dangerously, and she quickly lowered the tray to a table.

"Gale, look at me."

He was halfway across the room from her, but he might as well be touching her. She could feel him all the way down to the soles of her feet. "I'd better—uh, be sure Susan has enough blankets."

"If she hadn't, she'd have said something before now." He moved closer, and Gale took a step backward.

"The back door—I think I left it unlocked."

"Gale, *look* at me! Will you stop trying to run away? Didn't what just happened in there mean anything to you?" He was beside her before she could escape, and Gale braced herself to say what had to be said. "Saxon, I'm so glad your father is improving. I'd like to think Richard and I have become friends over these past few years, and I'll always care about him." And you, she thought despairingly. How am I ever going to get over you? "But I think it's time—"

"Yes, Gale?" He towered over her, intimidating without making a move. Gale glanced quickly behind her for a route of escape, and found none. She was neatly hemmed in by a bookcase, a floor lamp, and several pieces of furniture. "You think it's about time—?" he repeated silkily.

"Time? Well, yes. What I was going to say is that I mailed in my manuscript, and the new housekeeper's working out just fine, and Susan will be leaving tomorrow, and..."

He was stalking her like some hungry predatory beast, and Gale felt her temper begin to rise. Dammit, she was trying to offer the man a graceful way out, but if he insisted on forcing the issue, then they were both going to be put in an embarrassing position!

Suddenly, as if sensing that he might be pushing her too hard, Sax sat down in a leather covered armchair. "You were saying?" he prompted patiently.

Gale shifted her weight to the other foot. "I was *trying* to say that this would be a perfect time for me to start dismantling my darkroom and look for another place. Did I mention that I had been planning to move out even before Olivia left? Only someone had to stay. To look after things, I mean."

She stared at the muscle that was working at the side of his jaw. "Sax, if you go on grinding your teeth that way, you're going to have problems."

"Going to have problems!" He surged forward, gripping the arms of his chair, but before he could say more, she continued.

"I took the liberty of adding up what a commercial window washer would have charged," she said calmly. "When you figure in the cost of having the floors waxed and buffed, it comes to just slightly under what Mr. Crump gave me for the tea set and the chocolate pot, but without the—''

The sound that escaped him could easily have come from someone having a wisdom tooth extracted. Without anesthesia.

''Well, anyway,'' she said, not quite as calmly as before, ''As soon as Susan and Tonio leave, I'll be—''

''You'll be what?'' he said in a tone so ominous that she felt her lungs constrict.

''L-leaving?'' she squeaked.

''Over my dead body,'' Sax said flatly. Rising, he came around to stand in front of her, neatly boxing her in. It was a trap she'd been caught in once before. She'd made a mental note at the time to rearrange the furniture, but she'd never gotten around to it.

''Isn't that a little extreme?'' she asked timidly, dropping into a chair.

''I'll tell you what's extreme.'' Leaning over her, he placed one hand on each arm of her chair. ''Extreme is being so damned busy trying to salvage something that took three generations to build that you can't afford to think about your own needs. Extreme is watching someone you love hide behind a wall so thick you couldn't vault it with a fifty-foot pole. Extreme is—''

Gale cowered and he broke off then, a low, strangled sound escaping him as he reached for her and pulled her up into his arms.

''Gale, don't do this to me! Sweetheart, if I've made a mess of things, I'm sorry. I thought if I could just keep you here until things got a little more settled, we'd have time for us. I should have explained what was going on."

"Sax, I know you've been busy." She tried to be fair, but it was hard to be reasonable when all she wanted was to be held and reassured and made love to.

"I'd better tell you how things stand at the moment," Sax murmured distractedly, kissing her hair and moving his hands over her back as if to memorize each complex curve.

"You know what happens when we try to talk this way."

When Sax lifted his hands to cup her face, she could feel their unsteadiness. Turning her face into his palm, she kissed him, and he caught her to him again, rocking her in his arms. "Gale," he said huskily, "Don't kiss me—don't even move for a few minutes, or I'll never get this said, all right?"

She nodded wordlessly, and he began to speak. "I came home because of Dad—because we'd quarreled eleven years ago over his marrying Olivia, and both of us ended saying a lot of things that should never have been said."

"That Evanshaw pride," Gale murmured. "You two are so much alike it's almost funny."

He tightened his arms, and for a moment, said nothing. "Yeah, I guess we are, at that. I love that old man, Gale. But I left him here with no one to watch over him until it was almost too late. No one but you, and God knows, you almost got caught in the same trap."

"Do you want to be a little more specific?"

Sax stirred the fire. He settled them comfortably on the couch—Gale insisted on sitting beside him this time, instead of on his lap.

"It appears that Olivia's been putting off creditors for months, using Dad's illness and the confused state of his affairs as an excuse. Anyone else would have been cut off long before now." Sax laced his fingers through Gale's. One of his arms was across her shoulders, and she leaned comfortably against his side, her feet tucked up beside her. "Meanwhile, she's been transferring everything she could get her hands on to a blind account Benton set up for her at a Miami bank. The rugs, the paintings—those were all sold to an out-of-state dealer who's not too good at keeping records."

"But you thought I'd taken them, didn't you?" It had finally dawned on Gale that Sax had had no reason to believe otherwise.

"For a short while, yeah—I'm afraid I did."

She sighed heavily. What she'd done had been just enough to make him suspect far more, and just enough to make her look and act as guilty as sin. "When did you know?"

"That snide little IOU you wrote me, remember? If you'd stolen so much as a toothpick holder, it would have shown up on that thing. Believe me, honey, you're too honest not to make a thorough job of confessing when you finally get around to it."

"I don't think that makes a whole lot of sense, but it sounds just wonderful," she said, purring with satisfaction. At least it proved that in a crazy, roundabout way, he trusted her. "Actually," she said candidly, "I think I confessed several times—sort of. Only I was so anxious to get to the fun part—the forgiving and all that—that I might have been the least bit hazy about the details."

"To put it mildly," Sax said with a grin. "Anyway, by that time, Olivia's dirty little pigeons were coming home to roost. Those barrels in the basement? Those were to have been picked up and delivered to a warehouse in Norfolk, to be collected by the same dealer who bought the rugs and paintings. Mrs. McCrary'd been given instructions to let the men in when they came, only she was so stewed when they finally showed up she thought they were from the oil company. She accused them of selling us an inferior grade of oil that wouldn't put out any heat, and threatened to turn them over to the Better Business Bureau."

Gale burst out laughing, and after a moment Sax joined her. "If this weren't so—so tragic," she gasped, "it would be hilarious!" And she was off in fresh peals of laughter, tears streaming down her cheeks.

It was as if all the accumulated tension of the past few years had suddenly dissolved.

The door opened a crack, and Aggie poked her head inside the room. Her mouth was pinched in stern disapproval, but somehow, it failed to reach her large brown eyes. "What on earth is all this ruckus about? Are you two deliberately trying to wake the whole household?"

They sobered instantly. Gale's lips trembled, and her eyes were a little overbright, but it was Saxon who apologized. "Sorry, Aggie, it won't happen again. By the way, would you like to be the first to congratulate us? We're going to be married as soon as we can make the arrangements."

"Not a minute too soon, if you ask me."

"We are?" Gale asked after the door had closed again.

"I distinctly remember asking you. Dad asked you. We thought you'd said yes."

"I thought you'd forgotten. Or that you hadn't really meant it. I mean, sometimes in the, uh, stress of the moment, words get spoken that aren't really meant to be taken seriously." Her expression was grave, but the look in her eyes was unmistakable.

"My dearest and only true love, when a man gets to be my age without having taken the plunge," Sax said hardily, "it means that he's either too cautious to say things he doesn't mean, or he's not, uh, inclined that way."

"Sax, I'm not sure I understand what happened back there in Richard's room, but I want you to know—"

He placed a finger over her lips, and the gesture become a caress. "Shh," he whispered. "I know the most important thing, darling. I know I love you more than I ever thought I could love any woman. I know— I believe, that is—that you love me, too."

Gale remembered to breathe eventually. It took several minutes to tell him how she felt, for both found it necessary to pause frequently for a demonstration.

"Shall we allow Dad to think it was all his doing?" Sax asked, cradling the woman in his arms as if she were the most precious thing in the world, as indeed she was.

Gale thought about the train of events that had brought them together after all the years. "Perhaps it was," she said thoughtfully. In spite of all the pain and sadness, he'd come back where he belonged—and she'd been here waiting for him.

"Perhaps it was," Sax repeated, drawing her down beside him.

* * * * *

*...and now an exciting short story
from Silhouette Books.*

*

HEATHER GRAHAM POZZESSERE

Shadows on the Nile

CHAPTER ONE

Alex could tell that the woman was very nervous. Her fingers were wound tightly about the arm rests, and she had been staring straight ahead since the flight began. Who was she? Why was she flying alone? Why to Egypt? She was a small woman, fine-boned, with classical features and porcelain skin. Her hair was golden blond, and she had blue-gray eyes that were slightly tilted at the corners, giving her a sensual and exotic appeal.

And she smelled divine. He had been sitting there, glancing through the flight magazine, and her scent had reached him, filling him like something rushing through his bloodstream, and before he had looked at her he had known that she would be beautiful.

John was frowning at him. His gaze clearly said that this was not the time for Alex to become interested in a woman. Alex lowered his head, grinning. Nuts to John. He was the one who had made the reservations so late that there was already another passenger between them in their row. Alex couldn't have remained silent anyway; he was certain that he could ease the flight for her. Besides, he had to know her name, had to see if her eyes would turn silver when she smiled. Even though he should, he couldn't ignore her.

"Alex," John said warningly.

Maybe John was wrong, Alex thought. Maybe this was precisely the right time for him to get involved. A woman would be the perfect shield, in case anyone was interested in his business in Cairo.

The two men should have been sitting next to each other, Jillian decided. She didn't know why she had wound up sandwiched between the two of them, but she couldn't do a thing about it. Frankly, she was far too nervous to do much of anything.

"It's really not so bad," a voice said sympathetically. It came from her right. It was the younger of the two men, the one next to the window. "How about a drink? That might help."

Jillian took a deep, steadying breath, then managed to answer. "Yes . . . please. Thank you."

His fingers curled over hers. Long, very strong fingers, nicely tanned. She had noticed him when she had taken her seat—he was difficult not to notice. There was an arresting quality about him. He had a certain look: high-powered, confident, self-reliant. He was medium tall and medium built, with shoulders that nicely filled out his suit jacket, dark brown eyes, and sandy hair that seemed to defy any effort at combing it. And he had a wonderful voice, deep and compelling. It broke through her fear and actually soothed her. Or perhaps it was the warmth of his hand over hers that did it.

"Your first trip to Egypt?" he asked. She managed a brief nod, but was saved from having to comment when the stewardess came by. Her companion ordered her a white wine, then began to converse with her quite normally, as if unaware that her fear of flying had nearly rendered her speechless. He asked her what she did for a living, and she heard herself tell him that she was a music teacher at a junior college. He responded easily to everything she said, his voice warm and concerned each time he asked another question. She didn't think; she simply answered him, because flying had become easier the moment he touched her. She even told him that she was a widow, that her husband had been killed in a car accident four years ago, and that she was here now to fulfill a long-held dream, because she had always longed to see the pyramids, the Nile and all the ancient wonders Egypt held.

She had loved her husband, Alex thought, watching as pain briefly darkened her eyes. Her voice held a thread of sadness when she mentioned her husband's name. Out of nowhere, he wondered how it would feel to be loved by such a woman.

Alex noticed that even John was listening, commenting on things now and then. How interesting, Alex thought, looking across at his friend and associate.

The stewardess came with the wine. Alex took it for her, chatting casually with the woman as he paid. Charmer, Jillian thought ruefully. She flushed, realizing that it was his charm that had led her to tell him so much about her life.

Her fingers trembled when she took the wineglass. "I'm sorry," she murmured. "I don't really like to fly."

Alex—he had introduced himself as Alex, but without telling her his last name—laughed and said that was the understatement of the year. He pointed out the window to the clear blue sky—an omen of good things to come, he said—then assured her that the airline had an excellent safety record. His friend, the older man with the haggard, world-weary face, eventually introduced himself as John. He joked and tried to reassure her, too, and eventually their efforts paid off. Once she felt a little calmer, she offered to move, so they could converse without her in the way.

Alex tightened his fingers around hers, and she felt the startling warmth in his eyes. His gaze was appreciative and sensual, without being insulting. She felt a rush of sweet heat swirl within her, and she realized with surprise that it was excitement, that she was enjoying his company the way a woman enjoyed the company of a man who attracted her. She had thought she would never feel that way again.

"I wouldn't move for all the gold in ancient Egypt," he said with a grin, "and I doubt that John would, either." He touched her cheek. "I might lose track of you, and I don't even know your name."

"Jillian," she said, meeting his eyes. "Jillian Jacoby."

He repeated her name softly, as if to commit it to memory, then went on to talk about Cairo, the pyramids at Giza, the Valley of the Kings, and the beauty of the nights when the sun set over the desert in a riot of blazing red.

And then the plane was landing. To her amazement, the flight had ended. Once she was on solid ground again, Jillian realized that Alex knew all sorts of things about her, while she didn't know a thing about him or John—not even their full names.

They went through customs together. Jillian was immediately fascinated, in love with the colorful atmosphere of Cairo, and not at all dismayed by the waiting and the bureaucracy. When they finally reached the street she fell head over heels in love with the exotic land. The heat shimmered in the air, and taxi drivers in long burnooses lined up for fares. She could hear the soft singsong of their language, and she was thrilled to realize that the dream she had harbored for so long was finally coming true.

She didn't realize that two men had followed them from the airport to the street. Alex, however, did. He saw the men behind him, and his jaw tightened as he nodded to John to stay put and hurried after Jillian.

"Where are you staying?" he asked her.

"The Hilton," she told him, pleased at his interest. Maybe her dream was going to turn out to have some unexpected aspects.

He whistled for a taxi. Then, as the driver opened the door, Jillian looked up to find Alex staring at her. She felt...something. A fleeting magic raced along her spine, as if she knew what he was about to do. Knew, and should have protested, but couldn't.

Alex slipped his arm around her. One hand fell to her waist, the other cupped her nape, and he kissed her. His mouth was hot, his touch firm, persuasive. She was filled with heat; she trembled...and then she broke away at last, staring at him, the look in her eyes more eloquent than any words. Confused, she turned away and stepped into the taxi. As soon as she was seated she turned to stare after him, but he was already gone, a part of the crowd.

She touched her lips as the taxi sped toward the heart of the city. She shouldn't have allowed the kiss; she barely knew him. But she couldn't forget him.

She was still thinking about him when she reached the Hilton. She checked in quickly, but she was too late to acquire a guide for the day. The manager suggested that she stop by the Kahil bazaar, not far from the hotel. She dropped her bags in her room, then took another taxi to the bazaar. Once again she was enchanted. She loved everything: the noise, the people, the donkey carts that blocked the narrow streets, the shops with their beaded entryways and beautiful wares in silver and stone, copper and brass. Old men smoking water pipes sat on mats drinking tea, while younger men shouted out their wares from stalls and doorways. Jillian began walking slowly, trying to take it all in. She was occasionally jostled, but she kept her hand on her purse and sidestepped quickly. She was just congratulating herself on her competence when she was suddenly dragged into an alley by two Arabs swaddled in burnooses.

"What—" she gasped, but then her voice suddenly fled. The alley was empty and shadowed, and night was coming. One man had a scar on his cheek, and held a long, curved knife; the other carried a switchblade.

"Where is it?" the first demanded.

"Where is what?" she asked frantically.

The one with the scar compressed his lips grimly. He set his knife against her cheek, then stroked the flat side down to her throat. She could feel the deadly coolness of the steel blade.

"Where is it? Tell me now!"

Her knees were trembling, and she tried to find the breath to speak. Suddenly she noticed a shadow emerging from the darkness behind her attackers. She gasped, stunned, as the man drew nearer. It was Alex.

Alex . . . silent, stealthy, his features taut and grim. Her heart seemed to stop. Had he come to her rescue? Or was he allied with her attackers, there to threaten, even destroy, her?

*   *   *   *   *

Watch for Chapter Two of SHADOWS ON THE NILE coming next month—only in Silhouette Intimate Moments.

Silhouette Special Edition

COMING NEXT MONTH

#415 TIME AFTER TIME—Billie Green
Airline executives Leah French and Paul Gregory had a cool,
professional relationship. Then the dreams began, dreams that
carried them out of time, to faraway lands and into each
other's arms.

#416 FOOLS RUSH IN—Giana Gray
In tracing her missing twin, Erin Blaine's first find was dashing
Max Delany, her sister's supposed beloved. Dodging gunmen and
double-crossers, Max and Erin sought clues...and stumbled onto
unwanted desire.

#417 WHITE NIGHTS—Dee Norman
Whether racing down ski slopes or chasing the chills in a hot tub,
Jennifer Ericson couldn't seem to avoid hostile financier
Travis MacKay. Though he suspected her of pursuing him, she
was really only running from love.

#418 TORN ASUNDER—Celeste Hamilton
Years ago Alexa Thorpe, the boss's daughter, and Ty Duncan,
the laborer's son, fell in forbidden love, but family objections
and deceptions drove them apart. By tackling their history, could
they succeed in sharing a future?

#419 SUMMER RAIN—Lisa Jackson
Widowed Ainsley Hughes reluctantly brought her troubled son to
her father's ranch, only to find the Circle S failing...and aloof
Trent McCullough in charge. She'd once loved Trent's fire, but
could she trust his iciness now?

#420 LESSONS IN LOVING—Bay Matthews
Bachelor Mitch Bishop had much to learn about parenting, and
special ed teacher Jamie Carr was the perfect instructor. But in
the school of love, both adults faltered on their ABC's.

AVAILABLE THIS MONTH

#409 A CERTAIN SMILE
Lynda Trent
#410 FINAL VERDICT
Pat Warren
#411 THUNDERSTRUCK
Pamela Toth

#412 RUN AWAY HOME
Marianne Shock
#413 A NATURAL WOMAN
Caitlin Cross
#414 BELONGING
Dixie Browning

In response
to last year's outstanding success,
Silhouette Brings You:

Silhouette Christmas Stories 1987

Specially chosen for you in a delightful volume celebrating the holiday season, four original romantic stories written by four of your favorite Silhouette authors.

Dixie Browning—*Henry the Ninth*
Ginna Gray—*Season of Miracles*
Linda Howard—*Bluebird Winter*
Diana Palmer—*The Humbug Man*

Each of these bestselling authors will enchant you with their unforgettable stories, exuding the magic of Christmas and the wonder of falling in love.

A heartwarming Christmas gift during the holiday season...indulge yourself and give this book to a special friend!

Available November 1987

XM87-1